Also by Maureen Armstrong

ESSENCES OF TONGCHENG
HORIZONS IN TONGCHENG

July's Dream

BOOK 1

Maureen Armstrong

authorHOUSE®

AuthorHouse™
1663 Liberty Drive
Bloomington, IN 47403
www.authorhouse.com
Phone: 833-262-8899

Published by AuthorHouse 11/20/2023

ISBN: 979-8-8230-1628-5 (sc)
ISBN: 979-8-8230-1627-8 (e)

Library of Congress Control Number: 2023919718

The novel is a work of fiction. The characters, names, incidents, dialogue, and plot are the author's imagination or are used fictitiously. Any resemblance to actual persons, companies, or events is purely coincidental.

Print information available on the last page.

Any people depicted in stock imagery provided by Getty Images are models, and such images are being used for illustrative purposes only. Certain stock imagery © Getty Images.

This book is printed on acid-free paper.

Because of the dynamic nature of the Internet, any web addresses or links contained in this book may have changed since publication and may no longer be valid. The views expressed in this work are solely those of the author and do not necessarily reflect the views of the publisher, and the publisher hereby disclaims any responsibility for them.

CONTENTS

CHAPTER ONE

Onus

August 1994 Point of View

At home in my neighborhood decide on plans to travel far enough away from home but familiar enough to reassure myself of well-being. For past few years, struggling with making money-ends-meet and expenses with theft of life's savings, financial duress plagues plans for day-to-day security of health and keeping my apartment, or changing locations and looking for new place to live. Now, I know for sure to turn towards establishing a new home.

During my first trip to view land and buildings ambitions of relocating seem ominous few weeks ago. Weather drains surroundings of easy times with heavy fierce winds collapsing tent, or rain falls in buckets and deterring plan for trying to stay few days more. Now location decisions for more permanence descend into planning. In next days coming to decisions to choose alternatives to establish daily-living and being here or to relocate anywhere else, even overseas, varies between abilities to manage and refurbish buildings on land and other future options.

Though car trip through country roads seems different to weeks ago to find previous gas station, decide to pull over car on corner where busy truck stop sits in rural setting of ranching and hay crops. Stopping car and getting out to look at map in parking lot helps remove confusion of repeating trip to find identical gas station before becoming further disoriented and lost from driving to look further down highway for turnoff north to Sagebrush. After scanning state map for interstate highways from small rural community, find state highway north to Sagebrush in map and return to car. Turning car around go back down same paved interstate highway to turn right onto road driving north down the highway on interstate highway traveling from Missouri.

Familiar roads return to my view and community visited weeks ago emerging from vast country plains. Nearby, in large Nebraska prairie town amenities include good gas station and fastfood restaurant, and making stop in cartrip worthwhile. Staff allow sitting nearby at messy table beside magazine racks, and hamburger tastes great while taking break to rest from car trip. Though one hour later, and after feeling rested from driving, begin road trip quest driving several more hours. Country roads wind through Nebraska's spanning flat lands opening to vast blue skies and find interchange to state highway to Sagebrush and community closer to land and destination. As driving through east-west interchange up ahead emerge onto corner to franchise sign for popular gas station reststop for meal in late afternoon. Sagebrush community population attracts enough work and rural business in ranching, tourists or farming to be host to many services like hospitals or stores. After ordering coffee and sandwich make phone call outside restaurant.

"Sylvii, Carole calling from payphone at diner. I have arrived in Sagebrush, Nebraska from road trip from Missouri," Carole said.

"Thanks for calling, Carole. Nothing new here. Faith and Robert have not been in touch. Police have not called with any report of returning your money to your account. I am well, and glad you had a good trip," Sylvii said.

"I receive letter from Internal Revenue Service last week, Sylvii, with phone number for supportive help to file annual taxes by phone and set-up recurring payments of pensions to our bank account. I made this phone call to IRS before leaving and filed taxes. The account will pay expenses for apartment until we settle-up for new changes. My things still remain in apartment, and may have to be packed up at some point. I took couple stops along the trip for breaks and gasoline fill-ups. I am few miles away and close to final destination but felt I need to begin to call in to you to check on our progress with our complaint to police and let you know I am fine and safe."

"I am relieved. Thank you for calling from payphone. I understand phoning impossibility from your location otherwise Carole. Let's get together soon when you return home too," Sylvii said.

"Destination and camp set up with tent on new land purchase requires travel by car north from Sagebrush few miles away, and buildings appear usable but in need of lots of elbow grease for tons of clearing; though place seems charming in first visit to purchase three weeks ago, I am only able to do partial walk-through with land agent because of all debris laying about," Carole said.

"You, Carole, achieve many things with your suburban home in the garden and interior designing business. I believe in you," Sylvii said.

"My health care benefits came in letter last week, and insurance for health care extends into Nebraska, Sylvii. Doctors nearby in Sagebrush claim any of my health needs with continuing insurance policies, and local amenities include country doctor and small Medical Clinic. Sagebrush Pharmacy stays open on main street. I am feeling fine but trip through those roads seems a bit lonely. I miss your friendship, and am very grateful to you. Tell Wallace the same. Although first impressions of small Sagebrush community remain hopeful as a good place to start over, I believe overseas provides better security. Thanks. I must go now. Goodbye Sylvii."

In addition, Carole walks back into restaurant for her meal, sits down for their daily special of hamburger steak sandwich, and then walks over to cash register, "I will paying for coffee and food now," Carole said.

Driving away minutes later and down main street buildings look abandoned and beaten up for lack of care or paint with closed storefronts. Colorful flags of local schools and sports stars line main street.

Yet thoughts of wonderful times with Sylvii and Wallace interfere. Many months ago as Wallace guides set-up of second bookstore in resort community in upstate Missouri near popular lake and seasonal activities, Sylvii invited me to travel together to meet for few days and together determine choices for new locations as remedial relaxation. Disappointments with her own children, Faith and Robert, after Alain's death seems to be progressive and reducing her to someone without authority in financial and personal daily life.

Lunch with Wallace's invitation to lakeside restaurant in picturesque location highlights my own shockful of events that contrast distraught and daunting experiences at banks and my apartment I had shared with Alain before he passed on three years ago. We sat on the patio at the round table with Wallace's few colleagues in book sales business and Sylvii nearby.

Although providing momentary relief from everything in recent days with sunshine streams and vast, still, blue lake nearby, almost feel loss of Alain in a natural way with supportive people about. At home going to Mass with Sylvii past weeks brought about mutual hopes with others who felt obliged to share some of their own personal losses and grateful to Sylvii for speaking out, bringing her friend to Mass, and being part of their community of compassionate people. Any regrets felt surround my Baptist upbringing and need for driving long distances of five miles to simply go to church instead of local church down the street or a few blocks away. Somehow attending church felt welcoming but then Sylvii's community offers such depth of thought to include her friend in their local directory and offer her invitations to church picnics and holiday times. Sitting last Christmas with Sylvii and Wallace at Christmas Eve service with lighted candles, hold our candles sitting together praying for brighter days.

One particular church attendee, Iris, even discusses some sort of fraud created by financial planner signing her name with her agreements to investments without even asking. After losing most of couple's life savings, Iris's husband experiences health issues, a stroke I recall, and then passes away leaving Iris a widow, penniless like me too.

"Can we meet for lunch after Mass," Iris said.

"Yes. Today?" Iris paid for lunch at family-style restaurant where her story unfolds.

"Lost savings of cash with financial investments," Iris said, "and my husband told me his financial planner said he did not require his wife's signature to transfer our life's savings into investment portfolios. Fraud reports to police have no results for money for cash refunds, and continue to be outstanding."

Furthermore, Iris, like me, uses her monthly senior and pension incomes for keeping her apartment payments up to date, paying car insurance, and affording her few luxuries.

"Sagebrush is a good town," said neighbor from past in cottage country. Memories flood with thoughts for the well-beings of neighbors in cottages of beach community north of Sagebrush, and with trip to Nebraska. New awkwardness's invade old memories with abandoning problems with children, Faith and Robert. Leaving Sagebrush without stopping car again must arrive in daylight and final destination.

Exciting views develop glancing in distant horizons as spot property and leave the paved highway where oncoming traffic passes by. Turning left, drive onto gravel secondary road aching with thick mud ruts three inches deep and damp from recent summer rains. Crops ripening on either side of gravel road wait for harvesting season. Most often while driving few miles over gravel road billowing path of dust clouds develop visible behind vehicle rubbing raw memories of family with happier times in past years driving over similar roads. Optimism abounded for our comforts for family vacations or controversies amusing all with joyful exceptions.

Only this past spring, a few weeks ago, Fern's invitation to barbeque in park with Sylvii simplifies everything in our day-to-day relationship joys. Fern brought hotdogs and buns, and Sylvii picked up Dunkin Donuts and lawn chairs. Fern's portable barbeque sat on picnic table as we drank cold soft drinks, ginger ale or cherry coke, and flipped large hotdogs on her small grill on a humid, hot May afternoon. Sun beamed on us and over calm still lake as nearby children played in park playground, and trees brought shade from warm day's heat.

In spite of few remaining regrets in recent shocking daily experiences of confusing and disloyal children entertaining their own personal money needs, being here in Nebraska as a journey to igniting hopeful ties from lifetime memories and for being with others effects to push away sobering thoughts of holding close any family loyalty to children. In anguish of loss of their sense of reasonableness recall times of motherhood and young Robert seeming now bittersweet with keeping family's baby highchair for grandchildren even still useful as plant stand. Troubling thoughts compete with contrasting to a peaceful view in front of what feels like seeing with new eyes.

Two hundred thousand dollars gone from our bank account by Robert and Faith, they take without permission of parents by two adult children couples with their years of antagonism for cash towards their own father. After Sylvii describes her call to state office for public inquiries and guardianships, I felt at a loss as to how any of her plans change my losses. Sitting alongside local tennis court observing tennis game between Sylvii and Fern offends my senses for my personal security with sensitivities to recent experiences with banking and children forcing me to walk away.

Sylvii left the court and came running after said, "Carole. What's wrong, why are you leaving?"

"I am not wanting to sit watching any longer so took walk Sylvii. I left for a walk through the park."

Meanwhile the number posted at the apartment building for seniors quotes the Missouri State Ombudsman 1800 numbers to call in event of any questions to complicated issues. After calling and explaining story of children, Faith and Robert using a Power of Attorney to take money held jointly with husband, Alain, the agent for Ombudsman office repeated the phrases Sylvii shares she hears from Public Trustees office.

"Removal of funds from Alain's and my joint account we call, Theft by Power of Attorney, and a criminal offence to report to police," Ombudsman counsellor said.

After explaining our earlier call to police the agent took all my information. The letter from State Ombudsmen sent to me clears up any confusion these thefts create as to my own ability to manage such developments as loss of savings, and with supporting friends like Sylvii, and medical doctors confirming my own good health. Information of interpretation of theft appeared in letter to Sylvii she received last year from the Public Trustee's office. Statements in letter from Ombudsman declaring financial matters being secure with new bank accounts congratulates our steps taken for canceling Power of Attorney.

Moreover Ombudsman agent's letter confirms litigation costs to return my inheritance from husband, Alain do become client costs as agency will not pursue litigation on behalf of clients'compaints. So I am broke now with theft of Alain's and my savings with few options. Public Trustee's office suggestion for Sylvii's ability to try to help with applying for savings to be returned through conventional court applications for guardianship grow too costly and out of my affordable reach. What odd set of circumstances as I am the one who lost everything and the one evaluated for competencies when Faith or Robert show themselves off as stealing money from parents. After theft of life savings how can we apply logic for hopeful outcome, and Faith or Robert realizing their errors in judgment, from this Ombudsman for changing these financial losses to labeling criminal? Costs and opinions after Sylvii's meeting in the next community with Public Trustee agents help with nothing and only confirm I have become vulnerable to thefts from my children committing Theft by Power of Attorney during husband's illness. State police and even the FBI offer no immediate resolutions but do take my information with some degree of seriousness to investigate or with assurances from police and FBI agents complaint files remain open to investigate with offering their compassion in many phone calls and even meetings. Peaceful views in front in view comforts my disgraces, or without identifying myself as victim to crime state police officer advises.

"They are my daughter and son," I declare many times to myself and others, "How can they take my money?"

CHAPTER TWO

Faith and Robert

March 1991

Weeks earlier Faith linked her arm with Robert's arm as the two left the hospital.

"March weather seems like spring soon, Robert. I think we are going to lose Daddy soon," Faith said.

"I know, Faith, I am going to miss him alot. How about you and Mom? Are you preparing Mom for losing Dad?" Robert said.

"Well, you know Mom, Robert. She accepts the next day as normal like any other day, so I think she will soon adjust without Dad. We can manage all their assets with Dad's Power of Attorney he gave to us. Mom, I believe, will do well to go into some sort of assisted-living arrangement on her government subsidy."

"Two hundred thousand dollars in their assets left large amounts of cash too, Robert. So I think we should clear out their joint account, and let other medical people step in as they do in these sorts of situations.

Mom, we can be sure will be competent to pay her rent, buy groceries or look after her medical requirements on government subsidy. I think we will be fine. I've got some blank checks for Mom's and Dad's joint account. Shall we fill them in payable to ourselves, sign for each other as Power of Attorney with Dad's failing health?"

"Okay, Faith, I can meet you tomorrow morning about 9:30 am. Where should we meet? I have to get home to Cheryl now. She has plans, and our kids are coming at weeks end for their Easter break."

"How about dropping by our home. Rick will be glad to see you and our kids are away at school, and seem never to get home to visit," Faith said.

Next morning Robert arrives at Faith's and Rick's front door. Rick answers.

"Great to see you. How are you keeping up with all this mess with Alain's bad health, and your Mom not fairing well?" Rick said.

"With Faith, I am doing well and adjusting to losing Dad. We are going to look after the financial stuff this morning. Will we be in your way of other things?" Robert said.

"I am out in the garage doing some tidying before spring gets busy with lawn care, so make yourself at home Robert," Rick said.

Faith and Robert sit down at the kitchen table, and each fill out checks to the other for the same amount.

"One hundred thousand dollars can buy alot of stuff. What will you do with your's Robert?"

"'After buying ourselves the blue three quarter ton truck, we might go to Hawaii. Cheryl seems excited, and like a second honeymoon, *Ha ha*, and so on....'"

"Faith you must worry about the police being notified? You know Sylvii is close to Mom, and they've been friends with Dad for years in the neighborhood. Sylvii may wonder about this?"

"I would worry but I worked with those guys from our local police station in the hills and mountains of Missouri often doing missing persons cases together when I was still working as Conservation agent in the region. I get along fine with them, and if they check up on anything, they won't bother," Faith said.

"Yes Faith, I have worked with many line cops but Sylvii and Mom have been close for years, and Sylvii may decide to report our agreement as a complaint to help Mom. What then?" "Nothing will happen. I have got this Robert."

Across the city in the suburbs Sylvii enjoys long breakfast with husband, Wallace.

"I'm worried Wallace. Faith takes Carole with her everywhere and is always with Carole when she visits Alain. Alain is not recovering well from cancer treatments. I think we will lose him soon."

"What a shame. Alain is a great guy. I miss them both after leaving our neighbourhood and moving into that awful apartment complex with assisted living and that other meaningless stuff that only says we are all going to die someday and while someone we do not even know makes lifestyle changes for us when we might still be fine to do our own damn grocery shopping.

There was that great place with smaller homes near the mall and Walmart Centre. They both could have walked to get groceries instead, they end up eating other people's cooking, not even choosing the meals to cook. I know Carole wasn't doing much driving anymore. All that stress around them always with Faith or Robert. I told Alain to forget those Power of Attorney documents."

"Thanks Wallace. I have been losing alot of sleep over this. I talk to Carole as often as possible but when I visit Alain, she seems to act like I am the other woman, mocking me for the help with Alain's meals and such, or softening a pillow. He always such a dear friend, and feel sad about his health failing, and cancer treatments going nowhere."

"I really thought the building of their complex they moved to looked very nice, and people working their must be kind, but I agree, they lost too much of their personal freedom moving there in the exchange from house to apartment, and now Faith or Robert seem to be hovering around like charging animals ready to pounce. Faith called other day, and said how glad she was I had seen the building, as I went their with my church group last autumn. What a fluke of fate to lose our dear friends to some kind of family choice," Sylvii said.

CHAPTER THREE

Being Mom

1992

Undoubtedly like painful grones with the progressive speed of greed for pleasure, responding with loving gestures from Robert or Faith to mother, Carole, becomes contrary to usual family times. One bright and warm early spring day in days and weeks after Alain's death, Sylvii offers Carole trip to nearby Walmart for any shopping needs. After entering Walmart wide double doors both see Faith checking out groceries while shopping at supermarket igniting some normal loving past for Carole to walk away towards cash register near end of a long row of clerks checking customers' purchases.

To Sylvii their conversation looked like Faith said hello to her Mom in front of clerk at check-out at grocery story. Struggling with Carole's lifestyle chaos from recent findings at banks and for failure to pay rent out of Carole's joint account after tragic loss of husband, Alain, Sylvii helps and supports through Carole's grieving following days with errands like buying simple treats and groceries. Carole's and Alain's apartment manager suggests Carole spend few days in Sylvii's home for adjustment to being alone after death of Carole's spouse Alain.

Sylvii stands still in spot Carole left her from waits as Carole returns to her side and said, "Carole, what are you doing? I am not understanding your actions."

"It is nothing," Carole said.

"Your choice of course," Sylvii said.

The friends continue shopping for small bits of cookies or crackers, box of juice and stroll down clothing racks buying little except for one priced-to-clear pair of long stretchy jean pants for couple dollars Sylvii chooses.

As they stop off in book section, "Sylvii you have talent to write as well as any writer on this shelf," Carole said.

"When spare time makes writing possible I like to remember your encouragement to try," Sometimes I think about writing fantasy stories," Sylvii said.

Often since Carole's husband Alain died in hospital many weeks ago Sylvii stops in to visit almost each day. Alain passed away so suddenly from prostate cancer, Carole came to stay with Sylvii and her husband, Wallace, a good sort and help to Carole through difficult aftermath of shock, loneliness and distress. Wallace tries to support Carole with kind words and encouragement as he new Alain as well as he knows any of their friends or neighbors. Coming from the same suburb and raising families, they often took their children out to movie openings like the latest Bond movies. Gabriel, Sylvii's and Wallace's only son, remains close friends with Carole and Alain's children, Faith and Robert.

"One time," Sylvii said, "I recall Alain said, 'I wish better days and small things for you Carole and Wallace at our Christmas neighborhood celebration."

"Thanks for your patience with me Sylvii," Carole said.

Next day visiting and back at apartment Carole said, "I am sorry Sylvii. I spoke to neighbor in building who said I was wrong to go speaking to Faith at supermarket. I told neighbor of all your help at the bank too."

Besides.... Sylvii continues to attempt to drop by for daily visit with Carole in past month after sharing in Carole's new widowhood and financial aggravations now that seem criminal. Sylvii's work in retail sales and marketing taught many things to look out for in fraud opportunities with sellers and book contracts, but nothing seems as momentous as this. Calling nearby Civil Legal Office in Missouri for information after being with Carole for some of this banking activity from Carole's children seeming very brutal seeming as good response.

Agent at Civil Legal Office, Nita, said "This type of theft is criminal and we label, Theft by Power of Attorney. Calling the police agencies your best option. Otherwise, you can apply for advice to be shared financial partner with your friend, local bank may help or we can guide you through sharing guardianship issues with Carole from our office. However, your obvious choice in this instance -- do call the police. Please advise Carole and to help her cancel the Power of Attorney her children have with her, and to minimize any further thefts in this form, and one thing Carole must complete very soon."

"Thank you. Yes, after we left the bank, my friend Carole suggested we call the local police and we made the call. I expect to hear back in a few days as I left my contact information," Sylvii said.

Sylvii's and Carole's children remained friends from their own personal times together, and have been able to close to obtain more understanding of Alain's and Carole's children's actions. Sylvii shares Carole's events with husband, Wallace, and son, Gabriel. Gabriel, their son told Wallace that Faith and Robert advise Sylvii their father, Alain, told them they were able to enjoy the money otherwise inherited by their mother, Carole, and to take cash. So, Carole, of course taken off her guard suffers devastation, and now Carole must try to make adjustments.

Carole's children, Faith and Robert, also gave Sylvii a much smaller check and ask to visit at their home when Gabriel came for Alain's funeral and memorial. Sylvii deposits check into her account. Cashing check at her own bank but while helping Carole at her bank with details of financial adjustments and widow benefits from her husband's, Alain's, sudden death from cancer, bank representative Vivian told Carole about my check from Robert as if I had colluded with Faith and Robert to steal Carole's money. What a nightmare, as Sylvii later explains the check to Carole, and with her own confusion distress develops early for receiving any check from Robert so soon after Alain passes away.

Though by cashing this check her fearful thoughts develop out of sequence of events so close to Alain's passing away to cash to return money to Carole or use on Carole's behalf. Out of Robert's response to Sylvii's questioning, Robert denies wrong-doing with Sylvii's question to Robert of appropriate conduct to writing checks in circumstances after his father, Alain, passing away. Sylvii, as friend to Carole suppports Carole visiting in her home with her for few days and good suggestion from Carole's apartment manager, who operates multi functioning reception, for adjustments to new status of being alone and recent widow.

Then Sylvii helps Carole with her new financial issues as widow, like pension checks, and becomes involved in Carole's banking issues. Without interest in accepting financial gifts from Faith or Robert, puts the money after cashing check from Faith and Robert aside in her own savings, and begins to be Carole's own daily helper for resolving issues flowing their way with her friend. Carole, as Sylvii learns of events unfolding from Alain's death, determines to resolve problems for her old and best friend....Sylvii went with Carole to see Carole's physician after the bank gave Carole form to complete, and Carole's doctor refuses to fill in the form either as Carole can manage herself well enough, and with other's support. She and Alain were married many years, and of course Alain managed most of their financial business but like a lot of widows, now Carole must start doing for herself.

Local Trustee's office representative, Nita had said, "With supporting Carole you do well at this point to support or assist in Carole's crises. Keep supporting Carole through these times, and let the police manage the complaint. Carole seems to have abilities to manage and with your friendship assisting her. Thank you for calling. Criminal activities like theft by Power of Attorney must be dealt with by police. If at some point you want to become more responsible like guardianship with Carole with sharing in Carole's ability to manager her own financial conditions, then you apply to State's attorney or local circuit courts. Only as last effort as legal costs accumulate, and Carole does seem to qualify as being able to manage her own business and banking. Our agency do support your efforts for counselling and litigation in any of these type of situations."

Sylvii hung up her phone feeling at a loss of what to do next but strive for day-to-day events like grocery shopping at Walmart and offers support to Carole while meeting Carole's daughter, Faith, in Walmart.

Sylvii drops by to visit Carole and brought Carole up to date with inquiry to Public Trustee's office to discover evaluation of these events.

Sylvii said, "I think I understand your emotional pain with children and losses Carole. These days seems like money makes everything wrong," Sylvii said. "How about taking walk together through peony and rhododendron gardens?"

"I cannot guarantee my personal safety," Carole said as we stroll along pathway of peonies and rhododendrons in hot pinks and whites blossom on either side. "Keys to apartment Alain shared with Faith so making home available to others. Faith or Robert walk in at any time without a knock on the door. I feel fearful from threatening actions over money. After losing Alain or when I am laying in bed I now fear either Faith or Robert breaking in after all these happenings with money at our bank."

"Two hundred thousand dollar theft, Carole. We should call another police agency like the Federal Bureau of Investigation? I think what has happened to you this serious. Changing locks for fear of your life and calling local police are all fine. I think there is a hotline or something like this for a number to call. What do you say? You also signed Power of Attorney for yourself. I think something must be in place to help us. Can we change locks? Let's go talk to manager of building." Sylvii said.

Downstairs getting off elevator, manager's, Rhea's office nearby in lobby with open door welcomes anyone to stop in.

"Hello Carole," Rhea said.

"I'm glad to see you today. What can I do for you?"

"I wonder about changing locks on apartment door, or refitting lock for new key. Alain shared keys with

Faith and Robert so think I wish to feel more secure in apartment." Rhea said, "Our difficulties grow with changing locks as security staff around building require duplicate keys for building security as well. Costs grow with tenant demands so changing locks becomes issue of costs. After tenants depart often apartment locks rekeyed for new tenants become building costs. Our management recommends not sharing keys as our building security levels require inclusion in rent fees for insurance purposes."

Sylvii said, "Carole experiences high level of fear and anxieties without Alain. Without help from Alain or Faith without intentions of helping her Mom with paying rent as Alain had done all the banking, Carole's rent remains due. Carole asks for help with going to her bank and bank employee tells us in our meeting Carole's children, Faith and Robert withdraw all of Alain's and Carole's savings. However with Alain's good pensions Carole still receives income into their checking account to cover rent payments in your building Alain must have written before his illness, and unexpected death."

Rhea said, "Our apartment building offers exceptional security with personnel reviewing safety on each floor every night and morning. Security cameras on each floor track any activity in hallways."

"Alain enjoyed being here but gave in to demands for keys from Faith and Robert," Carole said. "Please understand Rhea."

Rhea said, "Building cleaning staff for hallways or apartments do offer alerts to management as they clean and supervise for usual activity for security measure ensuring safety."

Carole said, "We understand. We'll go now."

Besides before further arguments develop over Carole's predicament of loss and betrayals from grown children, Robert and Faith, Carole and Sylvii leave apartment building management office. Upstairs after departing elevator on fourth floor as making black tea, "Do you have fears Carole?" Sylvii said.

"Yes. Sometimes I think of evenings in bed someone coming into apartment like Faith or Robert and doing harm to me, or to you; their behavior becomes progressive police advise maybe with worsening threats or of violence or even physical things to you or me I fear, Sylvii," Carole said.

CHAPTER FOUR

Glimpsing Nebraska

August 1994

Yet tree line of property next to gravel road today stands as guide to find approach emerging from deep ditches of tall grasses off main gravel secondary road. Turning left off gravel today empty of traffic north or south, drive through frontage of thick tree line to land appearing, spreading in front and sticking out from tree lines of poplar and elm trees. Acres of property appear after turning left into opening in tree line. Driving over short road and approach to property through deep ditch growing tall grasses again discover oasis like olive groves to Carole.

Although spanning amongst broad acres of land buildings in front looks familiar like mine. After one visit weeks ago to view land and buildings decide to buy land and buildings with money from private account Alain sets up in event of sudden changes to our financial and healthy well-beings after sale of our suburban home in Missouri. Moving to Missouri to retire fulfills years of labor of work and raising family with two children in Nebraska. Two weeks ago as new owner, formulate plans to relocate out of Missouri to return to Nebraska and ownership where holiday times of past loyalties and times with neighbors found more joyful family life. Packed into vehicle useful tools for tenting accompany second trip.

Sylvii's suggestion to call the Federal Bureau of Investigation encourages me to believe in myself. What children do to parents can be wrong? Somehow Faith and Robert convince Alain to cooperate with their Power of Attorney, but I felt few reassurances. Alain seemed to know what to do, and he had been diagnosed early with prostate cancer. We both believed in his recovery. Alain never grew disloyal to his loving wife. Our coming of mature and older ages in adult life dictates our well-beings as intolerable as I ever feared. If I can set up a tent who cares?

Sylvii's trip into closest office of FBI in Missouri holds little promise last autumn.

Sylvii said, "No one I who met with Carole in an FBI office gave any clear news of criminal charges, or how your's and Alain's life savings to be returned. Meeting in waiting rooms with instructions to file reports with local Missouri state police encourages nothing in form of restoration of Alain's and Carole's life and wealth together and how they built worlds for themselves around raising one very good family with two children."

Summer parties at nearby Missouri lakes dwindles in recollection of fond times. Carole's son Robert loved meeting people in past lifestyles from Nebraska when holidaying in our neighboring state. Good past times with friends consume many thoughts and shared memories with Alain, Faith and Robert during cold, long, and of simple winter days and forty-hour weeks in careers and jobs in. Being young and involved in city life of after work dates in clubs or bars and daytime gatherings brought our small group of friends together. Robert's impression of Billy, so profound and pleasing to meet up this old friend, Billy, my old friend and later Karen's husband. Robert's tears gather as I explain death of Billy. I know his feelings from the bottom of his heart values others. As I share Billy's tragedy of workplace accident when the truck on the hoist collapses sends Billy to hospital, and later collapses Billy's lungs, Robert breaks down crying. Billy and I were close friends after I left Nebraska with becoming workplace friends with Karen and our other close friends, Yvette and Jessica while they still remain in Nebraska. We all grieved along with others but when Robert started to cry I felt the compassion a mother feels for knowing her child, Robert, as a decent sort in 1979. How did Robert develop these compulsions to steal from his mother and father, break into security deposit at our bank, and torment his loving father over money? We have been parents with family times. Criminal activity like stealing shocks me to my soul and outside the character of anything I have known or behavior we ever expect from Robert, our son? Monster-like to me now, Robert, and troubling to his father. Alain's pleasure of our Missouri lifestyle brought us to location closer to Faith's and Robert's new home state dwindling enough in day to day pleasures in our own home for Alain to seem withdrawn and nasty with Carole becoming impossible to share our home with. Alain cared for Robert, and often commiserated with Robert or Faith, as father's do, with cost of living changes or job changes and our grandchildren working in the next state or distances away, as happens with Sylvii's and Wallace's son, Gabriel, one day. Groceries and beef price discussions develop as costs rise above grocery budgets for everyone. Robert or Faith enjoy careers and financial successes in Missouri state conservation work but retirement attracts Robert early with less money for social habits and niceties.

One day soon after Alain passed on, and I stay with Sylvii in her home she shares with husband, Wallace. Our son, Robert drops by and complains about his next visit to the dentist costing him hundreds of dollars.

Three Years Before

Odd bits of jewelry become cushions to touch for decision to forego past of accumulations and memories of years of marriage and family. Boxes of necklaces and fancy earrings or lapel pins lay about. Fern meets with Sylvii at Carole's apartment and joins discussions in apartment on fourth floor weeks ago.

"These broaches with colorful glass beads feel like happier times in hand," said our mutual friend, Fern from our suburban street.

"I think if you feel like wearing any of these, please let me gift them to you now," said Carole. "Personal items as these bits of jewellery never will be in Faith's hands now."

"I did enjoy making you these earrings Carole," Sylvii said. "Even Faith seemed to share interest in crafting together. I guess she assumes more loyalty to become the thief she became likewise as Robert do instead of our friendship. I believe Faith's or Robert's assumptions doubt you and I together as friends form response to their actions and instead become children of such odd behaviors instead of as thieves, and out-of-character."

"I know," said Carole. "Even so I wish I had never moved here. What happened yesterday at the bank, Fern, when the financial adviser told us my children stole my money like thieves make it seem like the worst thing, so I wish I had never moved here. Both Faith and Robert's antagonism with Alain explained away often by Alain as the way things seem to be. I tried to make things fine, but they never were. At one time we were going to stay in Nebraska and forget about Missouri. Alain's dream of relocating to some sort of childhood fantasy in Missouri felt like good times since both Faith and Robert's moves to Missouri years before. Both enjoyed great careers in Missouri's Conservation offices."

Sylvii said, "Your home here you seemed to enjoy before moving you and Alain into this apartment. You know gardening and such keeps us happy. Visitors from France loved being with you and Alain in your home. Your house parties and meals together with company always exceptional Carole."

"Do you want to return to Nebraska or France?" Sylvii said.

Shaking her head, "I think travel abroad to France may help. I came from France, and Alain and I loved our trips back to visit few relatives."

"Where do you keep your passport, Carole? You did seem happy with friends and home in our quiet neighborhood," Sylvii said.

"Alain kept our passports in our safety deposit box at our bank. I must retrieve them from somewhere Robert or Faith have put them or apply for new passport. I can go to French Consulate to apply for passport from France if I must depart United States. Robert emptied the safety deposit box at the bank after Alain passed away. My passport seems to be missing."

"Sylvii. Alain need never to be treated as he was by Robert and Faith. He deserved their kindness, support through his health crises and respect from everyone. Those two tormented Alain with constant criticism," Carole said. "After moving to our apartment we both believed circumstances might improve, but the move escalated circumstances, and now we know for sure with all our savings being taken."

"Alain's health was poor, and Public Health met at hospital with us and Faith and Robert. I have little understanding about how Public Health operates. Antagonism towards Alain and I continuing to enjoy our home in independent style confronted Public Health beliefs of supportive medical or day to day amenities of supportive lifestyles into leaving and making adjustments for apartment lifestyle. We had to downsize from our suburban home to apartment building with options of extra services. Before we moved, Alain bought me a new automatic washing machine. Now I never feel like washing any clothes at all."

"In our recent visit before Alain became ill, Alain admitted Faith and Robert press him for Power of Attorney but only for medical-related issues. He told me he thought he manages to keep this Power of Attorney for medical issues only, and kept Faith and Robert separate from your own finances Carole," Sylvii said.

"Yes. Alain tried to share any wisdom for managing the decision for Faith or Robert taking over of responsibilities for our finances for medical reasons in their plans in Power of Attorney when his health seemed fine even before moving into our apartment. Moving from Nebraska to Missouri became our nightmare with both Faith and Robert living nearby in area,"

Carole said.

"I will take you to my personal attorney to ask for help. Will you join me tomorrow Carole? Fern you are welcome to join us as well for support," Sylvii said.

"No," Fern said, "and keeping quiet distances away but with knowledge of your progress creates an opportunity for me to be helpful in an objective fashion, offer advice, and be nearby too for any help I can offer."

"Yes," Carole said.

Sylvii said, "After we met at bank, Fern, Carole and I call state police. The officer took call and information about our meeting at the bank and results and of Carole, a friend, who asks me to call police on her behalf. I said she is very upset. The police officer on phone said he took my information in our phone call and someone from state district attorney's office soon to be in touch. We have heard nothing since."

Sylvii went on and said, "Anyway, I decide to call Faith. Wallace thought calling Faith might clear up some of this mess. Was their Mom's money reinvested, or was there a plan that we are unsure about? She always seems like a friend important in our son, Gabriel and life too. Between visits with you, sometimes we had coffee together and Faith often asked after Gabriel. Faith seems to admire Gabriel for moving across United States to go to Colleges in Alabama and Wisconsin. I thought of Faith as close friend."

In our telephone call Faith said, "Dad said he wanted us to have the money."

"Carole, I told Faith this cannot be accurate as your mother and father are close, and these funds were your Mom's to inherit," Sylvii said.

Fern said, "I do not know how you still stand living here Carole. You ask me to call up Robert to explain but when I call he refuses to speak to me, and shocking experience for his change of behavior. I ask Robert what was the plan, and did he have another investment he thought his Mom benefits from, like any popular annuity, or gold in Africa quick investment schemes. He offered no information, and so I hung up the phone."

"These emerald and diamond earrings look wonderful, so like you Carole in the garden. Diamonds hold values we believe look permanent, like diamonds-in-the-rough as they say," said Fern. "I hope Sylvii helps you in every way possible. If you think you want me to have these earrings, Carole, in time will wear them and speak at every opportunity of these dreadful times to anyone who listens. Carole, you truly are the diamond in the gardens of many wonderful times." "Fern, thank you, as I have not made any recovery from these troubling times," Carole said.

Next day in August Sylvii called and made appointment with her private attorney, Mr. George. Sylvii picks Carole up at her apartment to drive to downtown for appointment with attorney.

"Hello, Mr. George. Thanks for seeing us today and so soon."

"No problem Sylvii. I am happy to help. You were a good friend to my early start here and of our past business." said Mr. George.

"I was a new store owner in need of reputable attorney," said Sylvii. "Selling books and souvenirs created new chances for our family here."

Mr. George ushers Carole and Sylvii into large boardroom office and are seated together in a group beside large meeting table.

"My children took all our money. I went to the bank. My husband passed away three weeks ago," said Carole to Mr. George. "Sylvii offers to ask for help at her bank with joint account in both our names as I need support through this disaster."

"We will cancel or revoke any Power of Attorney existing Carole. I will draw up the documents. Sylvii can you help Carole set up new bank accounts? Go direct from my office to the bank when leaving here, close your account Carole you held with your husband, Alain, and make appointment at your other bank Sylvii for new accounts." Mr. George walked out of his office boardroom and came back in with pages of legal size papers.

"Yes. Of course. Right away," said Sylvii.

"Carole, any documents claiming Power of Attorney are revoked by signing here," Mr. George said.

Carole took the pen offered to sign. "I appreciate you doing this for me," said Carole.

"Sylvii. You need to go to the bank after leaving my office, and help Carole close her accounts and transfer money to new account at your branch. Faith and Robert should have no further access to Carole's income or savings," said Mr. George.

"Yes. We can go right away after leaving your office," said Sylvii.

"I am beginning to feel better," said Carole. "Thanks for seeing us today."

"You are welcome. There remains no charge for these services as I support you through this issue," said Mr. George.

Outside the office Sylvii said, "I will drive over to your bank with you, Carole."

After parking and walking in again to this same bank two weeks ago where all of this crises begins, Sylvii walks with Carole up to bank teller with making request.

"Mr friend wishes to close her account," said Sylvii.

"Are you going to buy a car," said teller.

"No. I am changing my bank account to a different bank," said Carole.

Outside Sylvii offers to drive to her bank across city centre said, "Are you up to continuing our business today Carole?"

"Yes, let's finish this today, and then I may begin to feel better, more secure in my apartment.

CHAPTER FIVE

Alain and Carole

Spring 1991

"Your rent needs to be paid Carole," the Manager said, "and we are deeply sorry. We all loved Alain and miss him."

Out in the lobby, Carole begins to feel unease.

"My rent. Of course rent must be paid. Thank you. I guess Alain took care of this. I will get you a check as soon as possible," Carole said.

Up the elevator to fourth floor, Carole picks up phone in her apartment and choosing number from phone list nearby calls Alain's and her bank. "I need to speak to someone about my joint checking account," Carole said to receptionist.

"One moment. I can put you through to Vivian, our financial planning representative."

"Hello, Vivian speaking. How can I be of assistance?"

"My joint account with my husband, Alain Laroque, pays out our rent but my husband passed away three weeks ago. My rent requires payment," Carole said.

Vivian said, "Faith called our bank and told us about her father, Alain, passing away. The bank shares in your sorrow for your loss. Faith mentions taking trip north to visit her son, and plans to return."

"Well, my rent requires payment," Carole said. "Can we meet later today?"

"Fine," said Vivian. "I can schedule appointment into calendar datebook for 1:30 pm."

"Good," said Carole.

That afternoon taking her vehicle to her local bank Carole picks up close friend, Sylvii at home to accompany her. Carole and Sylvii met years back when both became neighbors in suburbia, and always stay in touch. Now as old friends living in new neighborhoods, they often defer to or rely on the other one for support, help or sharing confidences.

"I really do not understand these events. Alain always had kept banking up-to-date, and careful with safety deposit box security keys in our nightstand. I wish I knew more," Carole said. Earlier at her apartment Carole repeats information in calling earlier and said, "Sylvii, I called the bank financial adviser, Vivian. She seems to be vague and argumentative when I asked about my account and complaint about the problem with rent not being paid. Something's wrong Sylvii. She said Faith called the bank to tell Vivian of Alain's death and plan for her vacation to visit her son, my grandson, Randy, upstate."

"Alain provided for you well, and loyal to you," said Sylvii.

"Losing Alain seems like enough grief." Carole said. "I am so grateful for the few days we have shared since the funeral Sylvii, and even staying over with you for many nights before living alone now."

Parking across street from bank in preferred parking lot for bank together they walk into small but popular local bank. Tall blonde, well-dressed in suit female bank employee meets them in bright waiting area of building we both, Alain and I know well from years of trying to make lifestyle choices like new cars and houses needing financing.

"Hello Carole," said Vivian.

"Vivian, dear friend Sylvii has come with me for our appointment. Will you agree to Sylvii sitting in on our meeting?" Carole said.

"Okay," said Vivian and leads down short hallway out of reach of row of tellers nearby. Vivian sits in large desk in bright corner office as sun streams through thin curtains with outside traffic noises close by. Please sit.

"Your account cashed several checks to family members with whom Alain gave authority. Sylvii, here, also cashed one check," Vivian said.

Turning with sideway stare, "Sylvii, what happened? Friends help each other."

"Okay, Carole. I did receive this check but the money went into my savings account to return money to you. I agreed to meeting with Faith and Robert three weeks ago at home only after Alain passed away. Robert called on telephone and asked to speak to me about their father and said, 'We want to compensate you for your loyalty to Dad."

"Robert and Faith came next day and met at my home. I was so confused but curious. Carole, I, of course, felt some confusion at this odd development, and said to Robert, "Are you sure of your ability to write me this check?' Carole, I did not understand either and felt such extreme anxiety for the meeting. I cashed the check, and keep money for you. Robert mentioned giving bits of money to his own grandchild. So I took their check," Sylvii said.

Vivian sits listening and staring at Sylvii as three women sit in sunny corner office. "With Alain's deteriorating health, Alain's children claimed their Power of Attorney," said bank employee, Vivian.

"That's wrong, said Carole. We have a joint account, and we benefit each other."

"Also, the bank safety deposit box was broken by Robert last month after Alain passed on. He said he needed Alain's will, and his Dad had passed on. You must pay to fix the damage," Vivian said.

"I should not have to pay anything. Alain keeps keys like safety boxes on our nightstand. in small container. What about all my funds?" Carole said.

"You can still use the account and government checks will continue to be deposited and along with

Alain's pensions and your widows' benefit pension check."

"What about the police?" Sylvii said. "Did you call the police?"

"No," Vivian said. "The bank estimates this as family issue not criminal activity affecting our bank." "I know Alain and Carole these wonderful couple benefit each other in event of loss. I am close to them both." Sylvii said.

The bank employer staring at Sylvii, "That's up to you Carole," said Vivian. "We did not call the police. Criminal matters are yours to deal with for crimes of a family nature here."

"Two hundred thousand dollars is gone. Alain's health failed but we support each other. If something happens to me then Alain benefits, if something happens to Alain then I benefit. Banks look after savings. You are responsible," Carole said. "We trust your bank to look after our money. How can this happen? I expect to pay rent as Alain and I have paid rent with Alain alive and well."

"Your children said, 'The government will look after you now,' " Vivian, bank employee said.

"This must be wrong," Sylvii said.

Vivian said, "Can you have your physician complete this form?"

Vivian hands over her desk one page form said, "Carole, Can you ask your physician to complete bank form and return to our bank?"

"Can I help?" Sylvii said. "I can hold onto form," and taking form from Vivian, Sylvii said, "Let's go see your physician after we leave here. He may be able to assist us."

Carole took form Vivian hands her but handing to Sylvii said, "Ok, " and with Sylvii left bank to walk through lobby to car across street in lot from bank. Carole said, "Sylvii, please drive."

Handing over the car keys Sylvii said, "We'll go to see physician in office down the next street."

Both women quiet as they drive few blocks from bank and go into clinic of several physicians said at reception, "Can we see Doctor Crawford today for emergency development?" said Carole and Sylvii to reception clerk.

After waiting few minutes in nearby empty waiting room soon receptionist leads us into Dr. Crawford's examining room.

"Doctor Crawford," Carole said, "We come from bank and banking representative gave this form as I need to deal with Alain's passing and our financial interests like paying our rent. Bank employee gave us her banking form to complete by my doctor. Our children, Faith and Robert used Alain's Power of Attorney and took all our investment funds. How can this happen?"

Sylvii said, "I knew nothing of problems, Doctor, but I was with Carole. We have only come from the bank now. Two hundred thousand dollars withdrawn from Alain's joint account to drain Carole's and Alain's account of investment funds."

Carole said, "Bank explains issue as Robert and Faith using Alain's Power of Attorney."

Doctor Crawford sits on table across small examination room and nearby.

"They did not have permission, Doctor, to take our money. I knew nothing of this."

"No, I am not filling this form out for bank," Doctor Crawford said.

Sylvii took the form and said, "We will go now." Walking out into quiet sunny parking lot Sylvii said, "I can drive you home Carole."

Furthermore as we enter apartment, we pass by building management office not speaking to building manager seated at management desk. After taking elevator up to Carole's and Alain's fourth floor large apartment we sit in small sitting room. Carole said, "We must call the police."

"Okay," Sylvii said.

On the phone nearby Sylvii makes the call. "I need to report a theft."

Soon officer taking call said, "Can I have the details mam?"

Sylvii said, "I am Carole's good friend and now sitting with dear friend. We have been to her and her husband's bank, and with friend who just lost her husband. Alain passed away to prostate cancer three weeks ago. His wife must pay her rent, so no rent being paid we went to bank to ask of details and for Carole to sign up for collecting government widow's pension benefits. That's when bank staff member told us Carole's children drain her joint investment account with her husband, Alain, and use their power of attorney."

"Two hundred thousand dollars from investment money. Officer, I am Carole, Alain's wife. I went to the bank, found my money taken, and children cashed checks to themselves and withdrew all," Carole said as she took phone from Sylvii. "This situation must be wrong or bank error. Can you look into these details?"

Officer Wilkins said, "I can forward your complaint to district attorneys for investigation by prosecutor's office to investigate, and with request to follow-through."

"Thanks. It's done, Sylvii, thank you and you have done the best and right thing by Alain and I. How can this happen? These are our children, my children. Alain never would have done this."

Days later, one afternoon Sylvii calls local state police officer, Wilkins and shares more information and continuation of call with Officer Wilkins.

Sylvii said, "We went back to Carole's bank again couple days later and same day after seeing Mr. George, an attorney familiar to our family business, and for Carole's needs for canceling any Power of Attorney held over Carole by Robert and Faith. 'Carole, I said, please walk to teller. I'm beside you.' Teller stands across us in cubicle in row of teller posts of bank.

'Carole said I'm closing my Joint Checking Account. My husband, Alain died. Teller said, 'Buying new car?'

'One thousand, five hundred dollars in account. I can write bank draft. Fine, said Carole.' Teller prepares banking details and hands over bank draft closing account." Sylvii said.

"Thank you, Officer Wilkins for taking our call and complaint. We, Sylvii and Carole walk out of the bank to Carole's vehicle, and I said, 'Now we will go to my bank on other side of city. 'Okay,' said Carole. So we went."

Officer Wilkins said, "I've taken down a lot of information, and will notify the State Attorney's office to be in touch. My transfer came through this week, but have transferred the file to State Attorney's office for someone in prosecution services to call you, as friend to Carole and Alain, or Carole."

"Thank you. I can share this information with Carole as we visit almost each day after Alain has passed away, and all these new issues develop," Sylvii said.

Days earlier, after meeting with Mr. George, and closing Carole's and Alain's joint account, very same day visit Sylvii's major bank centre, quiet in warm autumn afternoon with seating to waiting customers in lobby. The manager a man she had met before for her own personal banking needs seems amenable to assisting after explaining a few of Carole's developments for her friend's problems and from her own bank across the city.

"Let's sit here Carole," Sylvii said, "and wait until we find manager to help."

Sylvii walks over to teller to request manager, and returns to sit with Carole.

"Hello, Sylvii," said manager, male in mid forties. "Lucky to find me here on such a brilliant autumn day. Let's go into my office." Shaking Carole's hand said, "I am Mr. Forrest Carole."

Sylvii and Carole follow into small office nearby where Sylvii said, "I am helping Carole cope with some troubling developments at her bank. Carole closed her account, and my personal attorney suggests we set up joint account, like with Carole and I, as now Alain has passed on two months ago. Carole found out her children Faith and Robert drain her's and Alain's life savings after we visit her bank to settle Carole's widow benefits claims. Carole told me to call local police, and Carole made the complaint official."

"Yes. The bank supports this move Sylvii. Joint accounts between friends although not common bank cooperates with," said Mr. Forrest.

Manager draws out banking agreement and both Carole and Sylvii sign. "Okay. Looks fine," said Mr. Forrest.

"I am afraid we will have even more trouble," Sylvii said. "Neither Robert or Faith have shown any indication of correcting their invasion of Carole's assets and after their father's death.

Can you protect Carole? Carole requires all of her husband's widow benefits to pay rent. Some funds left help pay for small personal care like hairdressers."

"The bank puts red flags on accounts like this to warn employees to any odd or aggressive actions taken on account," Manager Forrest said.

Carole can deposit the bank draft from her bank to the account today, and then pay her rent," Sylvii said.

"All of this problem develops at Carole's bank we visit two days ago. We have been to Carole's physician Doctor Crawford refusing to cooperate to fill in banking form declaring any disadvantages in Carole's health. My lawyer, Mr. George told me to help Carole close joint bank account with Alain, her husband, very same day as canceling Power of Attorney, and to open new bank account. We make complaint to local police. I believe we do enough but with Faith and Robert, you never know," Sylvii said.

Banking manager, Mr. Forrest, pulls forms from an open desk drawer and pushes forms across desk to Carole to sign.

"We require your permission notice Carole to government to assign Alain's and your pension and widow benefits to your new joint account with Sylvii at our bank. These funds and our bank's request redirect any pension benefits for deposit to your new joint account. I can give you some blank checks to pay your rent and for immediate uses until such checks to your joint account with Sylvii return from printing and mailed to Sylvii. In that way Sylvii remains your partner in joint checking account, and assists with withdrawals from your accumulated income in your new joint account. Although our bank unable to assist with losses before through Alain's Power of Attorney any joint account offers you, Carole, some support and I believe protection from further losses. Your pension benefits covers your expenses and your current lifestyle in your apartment goes on as you wish. Your account's red flags attached to account notify tellers of unusual or fraud activity on the account. At this time check printing include both your name Carole with Sylvii as joint holders of account. I think you both have been clear with police about losses and I believe our bank supports all your efforts to return or respond to losses from Faith and Robert, your two children, Carole," Mr. Forrest said.

"I am beginning to feel better. Thank you," Carole said.

"Okay, I am to receive the checks to Carole's and my joint account in mail. Correct?" Sylvii said.

"Yes. Checks mail in next couple days to you Sylvii contain your home address. Are you definite about this plan because the only other option for bank means Carole's address to be added to account?"

"What do you think Carole?" Sylvii said. "I prefer my address with our names. I think as I am already a client of bank suppose the suggestion simpler but also brings up concerns about any influences over your banking income. Our level of trust as only friends remains very high concerns future or other prejudices with outside influence like Faith and Robert and our canceling earlier any Power of Attorney's held before. I feel someone may believe interference in affairs of family like the bank person, Vivian, may continue into this bank who said the bank does not like to get involved in these things and refusing to call the police.

The funds were in saving certificates owned jointly by Alain and Carole with checks written to Faith and Robert made from Carole's and Alain's joint account. The bank representative, Vivian, agreed to cash the savings bonds into their parents' joint banking account for cashing and writing checks to themselves. Even with Alain's health deteriorating if funds were required for treatment or care power of attorney written as medical needs for Alain's health care and for one, like myself felt Power of Attorney for medical needs, as Alain shared to me years earlier, safe to do this I believe. The Power of Attorney, with Faith and Robert, Alain told me about agrees to using for medical reasons. Alain went through weeks, months and years of aggravation over his plans for their parents' life savings, and then Alain's health failed with prostate cancer. Results like this and what happened to Alain and now Carole," said Sylvii, "seem very prejudicial. Will your bank stand up against this situation Mr. Forrest?"

"Yes, Sylvii. As these papers and checks indicate, you have a degree of accountability too Sylvii as joint owners of checking account. I believe you said your lawyer, Mr. George canceled the Power of Attorney held by Carole's children, Faith and Robert?" Mr. Forrest said.

"Yes, we went to Mr. George this morning and Carole canceled the Power of Attorney. Then Mr. George told me to take Carole to her bank again to close her joint account, and bring funds to my bank for deposit," Sylvii said.

"Sylvii helps me with these horrific details after the apartment manager told me my rent needed to be paid. I am so grateful to Sylvii, Mr. Forrest. I had no idea what had happened, and asked Sylvii to come with me to our bank. I stayed with Sylvii for two weeks trying to get myself together after Alain passed away. Everything fell apart for weeks before Alain's death with visits to hospital and Faith taking me about and to hospital for visits. Days before Alain passed away Faith stayed very close to her Mom as her Dad so ill, and maybe we lose him. Sylvii took me to visit Alain when he no longer notices anyone but sleeps. After Alain passed away, the apartment manager with kindness suggests to Sylvii I stay with her and Wallace for a week. I stay two weeks, and now things seem a bit awkward with losing trust in one's children for financial losses hurts my feelings so much," Carole said.

"I imagine Sylvii tremendous help, so with Sylvii's address on the checks we add comfort for even protection from any interference, even family members such as your son and daughter Carole," bank manager, Mr. Forrest said.

"Okay, sounds promising and Sylvii, thank you for your trust and faith," Carole said.

Next hour after returning to apartment building stop in to speak to building manager near reception. We here to pay Carole's rent and with helping Carole pay her rent with our new check Sylvii said, "Enough funds arrive from Alain's pension cheque for now I am assisting Carole with these checks from joint account between Carole and I, and a new account at my bank."

"Yes, the check looks good and rent paid in full for past two months. Congratulations for your good choices Carole," said Rhea, apartment manager said.

Next month one afternoon Carole called Sylvii on telephone said, "Sylvii, I share cup of coffee with neighbor in lounge area this morning. Of course neighbor said I must avoid conversations with Faith or Robert and she was so kind to suggest I set up postdated automatic checks to pay rent. Will you drop by later today or tomorrow to stop in at building manager's office to set up this arrangement?"

"Yes, of course," Sylvii said. "Carole, I am proud to be your friend and help and great news for support from speaking to neighbors I wish makes great deal of difference. I hope for your sense of feeling safe in your apartment building."

Next afternoon Sylvii drops by Carole's apartment. Sylvii said, "Carole you have come up with wonderful solution to writing checks for rent each month. Let's go speak to building manager."

"Thanks Sylvii. I am hopeful to look after some of my business now without Alain," said Carole. "My neighbor cautions me about being kind in situations at Walmart and speaking to Faith. I reget this and am sorry Sylvii."

Downstairs after getting off elevator on main floor down hallway building manager's office doorway opens exposing Rhea working at her desk.

—

Sylvii knocking said, "Rhea, do you have a few moments?"

"Of course," said Rhea.

Carole said, "I have been speaking to neighbor, another tenant yesterday who suggests automatic payments from bank account for paying rent with void check as easy solution."

Sylvii brought out one of Carole's checks to her account, now a joint account with Sylvii set up at Sylvii's bank after closing all accounts at our bank where Alain had done business.

"Sylvii helps me with business during this time," said Carole.

"Okay," Rhea said, "We can void one check and each month automatic withdrawals pays your rent Carole. Sylvii offers one check to Rhea across manager's desk.

"Will my rent be paid now each month," said Carole.

"Yes," said Rhea. "Your account with this check deducts rent in each month we receive your check."

May 1991

Later after sharing cup of tea in lounge restaurant, Sylii and Carole go up the elevator back to Carole's apartment.

Sylvii said, "Sunday is Mother's Day. Can I pick you up for Mass at ten in the morning? There will be short tea after services at the Church, and then I thought together a stop off at our local Gerome Park, time to reflect together and enjoy some nature?"

"Right. Let's do it," Carole said.

"Shall we go to Mass again next week or week after? I enjoy going so much but the drive may be too long," Carole said.

"I think you have great thoughts and suggestions Carole. I will love to pick you up for Mass. Going to church these past weeks good for us both. Putting our photos in the Church yearbook we share to view and memorable as conquerors of these unwarranted conditions." "The drive seems long to your church Sylvii. Sometimes the old neighborhood churches in Nebraska remind me of good times. I like our old Baptist church."

"I know Carole. Activities held at nearby baptist church seem like a very good idea. Let us go one day soon."

Next Sunday in May Sylvii walking into Carole's apartment building sees the concierge in front and said, "I am picking up Carole for Sunday Mass."

"Carole waits and sits in back loung area," said Jane.

Sylvii smiles her thank you, and wanders through to main floor lounge.

"Oh I am sorry Carole. I did not expect to see you visiting with Robert and Cheryl. I thought we were going to Sunday Mass."

"We can leave now," Cheryl said, "I think going Mass so great Carole."

Robert stood quietly behind the sitting Cheryl saying no welcoming words. Cheryl got up and walks out of lounge with Robert.

"Are you fine Carole? " said Sylvii.

"I am so glad you came this morning Sylvii," said Carole. "What a relief."

After the Mother's Day service Sylvii drives with Carole to local Gerome Park where both share in many good times together and with each other's families. They sit together on park bench watching many ducks in manmade pond. No words spoken, and day is cloudy with rain and cooler weather than Sylvii hopes for. Carole seems very quiet, and both glimpse at few women walking together down laneway of park.

Next day Carole calls Sylvii. "Sylvii, I am going to call police again. Weeks and now months seem to pass and no action. Will you come sit with me while I make the call and guide me through the results?" Carole said.

"I have been wondering the very same things," Sylvii said. "I will tell Wallace I am going out to see you, and I can be right over in twenty minutes."

Upstairs in apartment Sylvii and Carole relax after lunch.

"Okay," Carole said. "What about police?"

"Let us call again to Officer Wilkins's replacement? His transfer came through to another location within Missouri. On business card Officer Wilkins left number to call," Sylvii said. Officer MacWilliam soon answers. "Hello, this is Carole, Alain's wife. Have you got news of our theft of Alain's and my account from children and my information to Officer Wilkins?"

"Yes, Carole. The prosecutor's office investigate these matters," Officer MacWilliam said.

"What actions do you complete as no one calls," Carole said.

Sylvii took the receiver from Carole to listen to call.

"Thanks mam for your understanding. We believe Carole's written statement helpful to explain these details and ask if Carole able to provide written statement? " said Officer MacWilliam.

Sylvii puts down receiver said, "Officer MacWilliam will be in touch for your statement next week. Information Officer Wilkins took from me seems missing that was to be sent into complaint to State Attorney's office. Now he asks you, Carole, to complete formal statement and will come here next week on Tuesday."

"My goodness," Carole said, "I will do this."

Next week Officer MacWilliam, second state police officer to investigate, arrives at Alain's and Carole's apartment.

Officer MacWilliam said to Sylvii waiting with Carole, "Can we have privacy, mam?" "Officer MacWilliam asks for privacy Sylvii. Can you wait downstairs while we speak Sylvii," Carole said.

Sylvii said, "I'll wait in lobby."

In Carole's apartment as Sylvii joins Carole later, Carole said, "My statement went like this Sylvii, 'I went to the bank, found my money taken, and children taken all money. This situation must be wrong or bank error. Can you look into these details?' I told Officer MacWilliam everything."

"Four thousand dollars remains available in my savings account, Carole, for litigation costs. When I went to speak to Officer MacWilliam after our phone call, I told him about this check from Robert. The costs of trying to apply for guardianship or to help support you as becoming vulnerable to your own children seem high, but I did check with one attorney. Those receipts from paying lawyer for advice I gave Officer MacWilliam when Officer MacWilliam called me to speak to him at the police station. The officer asked me to return to your bank for the canceled checks of the funds stolen. So I followed his advice."

"Two hundred thousand dollars written in checks to Robert and Faith now become evidence. I had to return to speak to second bank employee, Nancy. Her help became immediate."

"One thousand dollars left in savings funds Bank Manager Forrest offers to invest for you now."

"My goodness, oh my God Sylvii. Thank you. I feel weak and speechless," Carole said. "Four thousand dollars plus smaller amount of check Robert gave me I spent on lawyer for advice to assist with gaining some authority in your financial well-being and advice from Public Trustee's office. Your doctors, Carole and both family doctor and even psychiatrist we visited together last month, confirm your health," Sylvii said back in Carole's apartment.

"I think we must call the police or state prosecutor's office again. I'm afraid, " Carole said.

"Yes, I agree. The bank duty is to you for your trust to look after Alain and you, Carole and your shared money," Sylvii said.

Next day Sylvii picks Carole up in morning at her apartment. "I feel tremendous relief," Carole said.

"I am glad we got legal help as soon as possible Carole. After our meeting with your banking adviser I went home and found sleep difficult. I felt fear of my own because I have known Faith and Robert so many years. I had never imagined them able to do anything like this to you," Sylvii said.

"They tormented Alain alot. No one should have gone through what he did. I wish I had known more. Only thing I recall saying you should obtain legal separation because I thought your health was effected, and I around often enough when Alain became so cranky with you without any real cause. His disrespect troubled me so much. Even your health seemed affected when I visited you in hospital. Gabriel came with me and said so too. Wallace, although supportive, said little about anything at that time. He seemed distant with trying to establish and support the second store owners in the other location."

"When I confronted Alain with not being able to continue as we were, and I even told him Sylvii advised me to get a legal separation. My health fails and Sylvii and Gabriel visit in hospital. He told me how Faith and Robert torment him for control of money, selling our home, or anything to do with taking money from us. That's when he told me how when he was alone with Faith or Robert he hears complaints about me, their mother, and how their own money requirements means he needs to give them legal authority," Carole said.

"Alain was more confident lately, and when you sold your home I think Alain enjoyed the apartment somehow with more time for easier activities than yard maintenance but maybe that was only my impression, and some reprieve because no longer was your equity in your home available," Sylvii said.

"We gave Faith and Robert financial gifts after selling our home in the suburbs, and the apartment costs became so much less. Alain's income was good."

"I do recall the day we talked together with Alain and Wallace before moving out of our neighborhood. I felt sort of sad I think as Alain said to me you know Sylvii, Carole does not qualify for any government social funding. I thought he was deliberate in his intentions to respect and provide for you, but now I wonder of Alain's many fears of losing you to legal separation because of Faith and Robert by making declarations for his money the real cause."

Sylvii refuses to share call with Carole one late Friday afternoon from litigation and guardianship attorney with threatening advice of hearing from criminal attorney for Faith, and the same State Conservation Office hires. The letter threatens Sylvii for receiving financial gifts from Alain. This humiliation goes beyond her own imagination, a complete lie, and offers little hope for helping Carole. Canceling the application for court guardianship for vulnerable adults and must be dropped.

"Now, Wallace wishes to avoid any of this controversy with me, and I think his emotional distances from me scary too. He refuses to discuss your situation. Carole, I am proud to be your friend and help and great news for support from speaking to neighbors. I wish everything we do makes great deal of difference I hope for your sense of feeling safe in your apartment building. Carole you have come up with wonderful solution to writing checks each month. Let's tell Fern. I think she will be so pleased."

Later Carole meets Fern and Sylvii at Fern's home.

"Thanks Sylvii. I am hopeful to look after some of my business now without Alain," Carole said. "Fern, checks from my monthly pension checks now remain in joint account with Sylvii set up at Sylvii's bank after closing all accounts at our bank where Alain had done business."

"Fern, Sylvii helps me with business during this time," Carole said. "After meeting with apartment manager, Rhea said okay, and accepts void check from our joint account. Sylvii offers Rhea my void check as she sits across her manager's desk. Will my rent be paid now each month we ask? Yes, your account on this check will deduct rent each month."

Later, back at Carole's apartment, Carole and Sylvii need to call Officer MacWilliam and share Mother's Day. After going up the elevator Sylvii makes call to Officer MacWilliam sharing update of Mother's Day. He wonders what Robert was like…

"I told him he did not say a word but stood behind Cheryl not speaking," Sylvii said. back to visit at Carole's apartment with Fern another day, and sharing her call with state police officer MacWilliam of last Sunday Sylvii had said, 'In two Sundays we celebrate Father's Day. Can I pick you up for Mass at ten in the morning? There was short tea after services at the Church, and then I thought together again for a stop off at our local Gerome Park, time to reflect together and enjoy being out in nature.'

'Right. Let's do. Father's Days seems like one and our lonely struggles. One after another after children grow into their adult lives, and enjoy their own pursuits. Losing my own son, Gabriel to his career brings pleasure for everyone, but I want to remember how Gabriel helped me feel like his valuable Mom with his day to day good nature Sylvii said.'

'We go to Mass again next week or week after? I enjoy going so much but the drive may be too long, Carole said, and I think you have great thoughts and suggestions.'

'I will love to pick you up for Mass. We can try another church closer to home too, Sylvii said.' I told Office MacWilliam as much as possible he listens to.

Then......third Sunday in June Father's Day

Walking into Carole's apartment building sees the concierge in front and said I am picking up Carole for Sunday Mass. Carole waits and sits in back lounge area said lounge concierge, Jane. I wander through to main floor lounge then see them. Robert and his wife, Cheryl, sitting near Carole.

"I am sorry Carole. I did not expect to see you visiting with Robert and Cheryl thought we were going to Sunday Father's Day Mass," Sylvii said.

"We can leave now. I think going to Mass so great Carole," Cheryl said.

Robert again stood quietly not speaking behind Cheryl sitting across from Carole and saying no welcoming words not even hello. Cheryl got up and walks out of lounge with Robert.

"Are you fine Carole?" Sylvii said.

"I am so glad you came this morning Sylvii. What a relief. They show up for these visits, and I sit but say nothing."

Next day Carole calls Sylvii, "Sylvii, I am going to call police again. Weeks and now months seem to pass and no action. Will you come sit with me while I make the call and guide me through the results?" Carole said.

"I have been wondering the very same things, I will tell Wallace I am going out to see you, and I can be right over in twenty minutes," Sylvii said.

Soon in Carole's apartment, in conversation on phone, "What was Robert like?" Officer Macwilliam said.

Sylvii said, "He did not say a word. I was stunned."

CHAPTER SIX

Carole's Diary

August Sunset at 8 pm 1994

Conditions light enough with daylight and sunsetting to settle in.

I arrive at the *Olde Homestead* at 6:04 pm. Tent set-up took about one hour and camp set up with small meal forty-five minutes. The trip was a bit far south on highway but the road was smooth and much less traffic. A bit of gravel with lots of dust develops on the secondary road but no traffic.

After only viewing photographs of buildings and land from a distant place and Missouri home, feel somewhat deflating confidence in my physical abilities as see the clean-up ahead. The many purple thistle blossoms look like blossoms in seed and seem to be everywhere. I imagine being able to pull them all.

I see toolshop, and know I still want to try to make sense of refurbishing potential uses. The old but attractive looking vintage-style double doorway with one

---

door half torn off hinges hides interior in photograph. Weeks ago salesman walks me through knee high deep dirt and unknown quantities of mess. Projecting success of relocating to useful shelter although looks simple enough with sweat and ambitions.

Later resting inside the tent in sleeping bag on dry plastic mat, determine options, write notes, and develop plans for day's ahead. Driving anywhere seems easiest, so plan on going to city next day. Directions from salesperson to local library with purple paint on corner building down main street helps along progressions of planning for next day. As my Visa delay circumstances grow to travel abroad to return to Thailand to teach English as a foreign language, I will try to stay the month of September. I brought warm clothes and make coffee with fuel and propane stove.

01 September

My first day begins mid-morning at 09:30 am., when I view the very old barn in more detail. I walk through the front door which I had not done before. The hanging door looks insecure so I had chosen only to walk in through the back door. The front of the barn seems to contain approximately six stalls. In between each stall is a curved fixture which sits about head level and looks like a very thick hook to hang a coat on. There is a valley walk-way or a long alley in front of the stalls resembling a feed or run-alley. The left side of the barn seems more compact than the right

—

side. Possibly different types of animals were housed as in a mixed farming barn with pigs, chickens, horses and cows.

The back of the barn separates from the front of the barn with one-half wall for any animals after leaving the barn for back pasture or yard area. From the back of the barn access ladder with stairs like narrow boards nailed to exterior wall from barn's concrete floor.

In front of ladder must move one pole with handle and flat, rectangular shovel attached to pole ladder univiting exploration above. Barn's past days kept shovel like a pitchfork for moving hay around.

Lump in throat for physical fear gulp away all, with notebook in front pack around waist, whistle to call for help and flashlight limb onto the barrier fence between the alley and the last stall in the front section to step onto the first rung. Height of ladder steps look very high set apart like any every kitchen ladder.

After climbing up these narrow boards, take pictures taking camera from backpack easy to rest on floor of upper level by pushing head through square opening in floor at top of these ladder rungs.

Looking up through man-made opening into the second storey, hay covers floorboards looking attractive in daylight almost like hardwood flooring in any home but with yellow scattering over second storey. Taking mental note but writing in notebook, some floorboards missing from floor create create gaps in floor as look across the floor opening on upper level, before climbing down.

Taking walk into the backyard smaller pasture area of the barn breathe in fresh air in back acres of land with open views of land in crops around back acres outside of barn. Weaker in arms and legs with effects of climb and viewing barn write notes as reminders of exhaustive work for visiting up level in barn for impressions of durability and usability filling pages with sketches and images of past carpentry and farm work.

Past owners plan for their barn to house variety of animals including sustenance like hay crops, and maintaining hay loft. Outside walking towards the back fence twenty feet from barn's back door, stretch muscles in arms and legs after climbing through barn.

Leaving country to go overseas, and keeping the new acres of property occurs to me as simply fine, and to need to consider ignoring any frustration with all work but plan to establish new life here on land in Sagebrush community. Someone of past creating very large find interesting structure called a barn, even with a newer sheet metal roof to provide longevity.

Issues to consider are:

Do I want to sell the barn?

Develop the barn into any usable building?

Sell the old wood?

Fantasizing to develop permanent home from barn and look for options in some sort of extravagant plan for a home with first-level bathroom, kitchen, living area and upstairs into two bedrooms make barn visible attraction from roadway through countryside across many acres of flat land. Check for architect in Nebraska at local library? Contact in short call from payphone in Nebraska to expert in architecture.

September 7 pm

Next day in the afternoon I took a drive to find nearby lake in view from front gravel road and about four miles from driveway. Possible considerations include boating with aluminum and very light canoe and to be carried to lakeshore. Today lake appears to be attracting wildfowl such as geese flying above.

In the drive down the country road, two hawks each sit kitty-corner from each other on fence posts. The hawks were as large as footballs, grey with spots or splotches of whites.

Farm road to nearby lake grows waist-high ripened wheat and simple dirt road appearing for tracks of single lane like in the middle of nowhere.

02 September

Sustenance with writing simple verses.

03 September

...and then writing again next day.

04 September

After hot tea and cereal, leave for beach resort at 11 am. Driving through city nearby few memories evolve with fried chicken restaurant fresh and sharp looking but popular pizza place missing from last memorable spot visiting with friends many years back.

Stores arrange themselves in downtown core with trendy shops here and but with now street empty of past small grocery mart, or department stores with lunch counters. Market store owner selling us many pounds of ripe bananas long disappears from main street. Driving further east find on city's edges, memories from more recent days and fast food places where we celebrate birthdays with cupcakes and burgers.

Leaving small city-size town, I drive for miles to beach and village to find memories of family birthday parties or folks and places like keepsakes of trends to follow as when Beatrice said, "How do you enjoy restaurant cupcake with sizzle candle?"

After stopping car nearby of past beach homes on street where with friends, Beatrice and Carl, enjoying many summer vacations. Cottages look similar to small homes and street carries trickle-trends of memories and visits about parties with cupcakes or seasonal popular music.

More than that after stopping car on side of quiet unpaved lane, bring out camera and to take pictures of sultry dark, sandy lane where our relic of small house sits. Here and there trees of poplar and spruce planted by Alain from our past summers continue to grow. Whoever dwells in former cottage these days tends trees taller than cottages now as mature trees in front and back to continue growing.

Small resort cottage still stands but more modern-looking renovations adorn small home now looking cute like a cottage with pretty white siding and white roof. Compulsions for few more photos to record this visit to recall past summers with friends or families ignite spirits of calm before stopping in front of Carl's and Beatrice's place few cottages upstreet.

I see out of state licence plates, and stop in front to chat said, "I knew owners twenty years back, and visiting area. How are Carl and Beatrice?"

The owner, standing nearby with bag of produce purchases she sets on outdoor patio sofa stops her activity, and taking time said, "Carl passes on two years ago but Beatrice reports health as being very well and in fine health."

I said, "I bought place with land fifty miles south and with some simple but very old buildings."

"Oh, those locations are the best," she smiles.

"Thanks," I said, "I seem to retain mysterious beliefs of realizing some kind of future in area. I recall Carl dreaming of visiting Thailand. I worked years ago in Thailand and waiting to return very soon."

Female owner of middle age offering no self-introduction said, "Carl and Beatrice sell them their comfortable cottage and summer home more than twenty years ago. Together Carl and Beatrice stop in ten years ago to see the old place."

"Great to speak with you, and thank you for updates on Carl although so sad," I said.

"Carl suffered with cancer and few other ailments," new owner said.

After farewells, and thanking owner for this important information, in spite of sad news, drive away with deep fortitudes to explore on going to public sandy beach. Large parking lot in front of sandy beach and playground remains clean and kept with garbage cans and picnic tables to welcome public visitors.

Parking car in empty lot assume best and worst of trip. Losses of older friends, changes in ownerships of cottages with years passing, decide knowledge of location valuable to changing circumstances. In bag towel, sketch and writing pens and paints fit well and in backpack camera remains like old friend as special gift from Alain many birthdays ago for to be taking many more photos up and down shoreline.

Sitting down with beach towel covering white sand, open up back pack for supplies and thermos for water and few items to pencil sketch and write poems in journal calling, "fourth of September". After sketching out with water colors lake and shoreline in front, enjoy windy walk of summer winds, foot high waves and shoreline of pelicans swooping for photographs.

Side-by-Side Buildings

8 p.m September

Writing into journal book plan objectives for continuing to establish securities of shelter out of harm and of weather patterns:

Clean-up in the tool shop entrance work area and side building worthwhile to continue. Concrete opening exposes flooring underneath layers and layers of dirt and refuse not clearly visible but looks like insulation blowing in and out of walls.

04 September 8:30 in morning

Laying in tent in early morning warm sunshine peek out flap and see sunrise shining on old wood but inside broken doorway to building. Attractive light in squares forces way into abandoned building filled with dirt from years of neglect. Lighting looks attractive in style from shape of windows to decide to get out of warm sleeping bag, dress in work clothes like old sweats with no other use in mind and Tshirt with thin jacket, and take camera out of car safe and left in dryer spot like the backseat.

Years back in easier times with Alain purchasing thirty-five millimeter camera as extravagant gift for special birthday celebration and thought, decide on our future together with children and travel. In this remote place surroundings offerings with acres of crops and overgrown grasses, early this morning now begin to photograph sunshine in blocks of squares and images like polka dots shining through high square windows of abandoned dumpy room.

Laying in sleeping bag of tent this morning continue to imagine opportunities from seeing glimmers of chances on unpainted walls from brightness of sun's rays set into square blocks from windows without panes of glass cut out of wall across floor area of dirt. Tools for cleanup include shovel brought along with tent supplies utilizing for sweeping.

"Stop." Carole said to herself.

Stopping to photograph light on wall, grab slice of bread and juice-box from box of food in car, put camera safely out of way under passenger car seat, take keys from waste band, and drive few miles into Sagebrush.

Gas station with hardware sits on edge of town. Gas attendant comes out to fill car, and must go into gas station to pay clerk. Inside are several useful items. Good solid broom and locks for granary storage cost thirty dollars, plus gasoline. Expenses add up and note these for investment costs in small notebook from purse.

Gasoline $35

Shovel $15

Locks $10 Total costs $60

Driving back to acreage efforts materialize from plan with purchasing simple tools. Although Alain kept most of our books of financial business, now on my own know without a doubt of importance to know these things and costs of choices, purchases and create new and details in effort to stay on now refer to as *Olde Homestead.*

Back at *Olde Homestead* work starts at eleven in the morning and stop for day at two in afternoon. All of the debris from right wall clutters floor and thick with dust. Stuff seems unrecognizable but after uncovering layers of blown in dirt find unsealed thick iron long rod with hook for shiny, old crowbar.

In removal project bring shovel brought along in car grab from trunk. Now, shoveling with tools and use of garden shovel, shovel all dirt or debris covering floor under high metal apex roof decide to carry debris by

—

shovel to pile on top of uncut grasses in field to left and outside of building covering tall grasses left growing.

Broken boards lay in front of opening in wall exposing nails frightening as threats to physical safety for fear of cuts or scrapes from broken vintage opening in wall with one hanging door off of years of useful hinges. Open doorway allows fresh air but in front find remnants of boards, maybe from doors broken off of hinges still exposing themselves on frame of opening, laying about in grass.

Thinking about any glimmers for reusing imagine boards responding to cleaning and expose tongue-in groove permances, Alain and I used to admire in garage or rummages from buildings, in solid wood, almost like oak. Keeping boards for useful projects may include patching missing areas in walls.

05 September

Next day plan to relax and escape with visit to city. Thirty minutes' drive over gravel onto paved highway covers twenty miles or less. Mainstreet appears with restaurant, bank, grocery store and small corner building. Parking on street out front wander in and meet smiling librarian.

"I have country place south a few miles. Can you issue a new library card?" I said. Librarian said, "Yes, and our library availability extends to discover books available from vast area brought in from around the State upon request.

"Wonderful," Carole said.

"Please fill in form. Of course identification requirements like property location and driver's licence fine."

"Here. I have my out-of-state driver's licence, and property tax details," Carole said."Looks fine. Thanks. Here is your new library card," librarian said.

"Thank you," and put new card in wallet next to driver's license.

Outside local library holds phone directories for upstate architects contact one, Architects for Rural Bulding. In short call from payphone outside library to expert in architecture from upstate advises against starting project with old wood.

Architect said, "To take down wood to beams and build up from foundation costs accumulate for cleaning wood of bugs."

After personal win of new relocation detail like access to library, return to *Olde Homestead*, and sit with tea to mourn the loss of the old friend, Carl, without any hope of seeing or visiting again.

Our stories sharpening edgy spirits of past comforts with qualities of returning to our past to write notes on thick bits of journal paper of Carl and Beatrice....

To tell a bit of our stories eases with comfort but rawness here of simple survival appearing as writing on pad of thick pages by writing stories while laying on sleeping bag in tent. Sunset at 8 pm.

05 September and 06 September

Progress Report
Measurements taken: workbench is twenty feet and begin with restoration.

8 pm First Sweep 07 September

Slow morning to enjoy long breakfast in sunshine with bagels and peanut butter for recall better days write journal entries. Remembering visits this past month since returning from Thailand recall from reading notes for warm thoughts as joyful:

Extravagance of past weeks and of seeing the art and crafting exhibits in large city with friends continues to stick with me. Riding in backseat with their child and watching facial expressions for darkness driving through dark tunnel appear with shock–dismay on small face. In our pleasant visit while I speak to child speaking with sound said, "Tsk tsk."

Baby said, "Tsk tsk.

Today clean-up project begins at one thirty in afternoon, and ends at four thirty in afternoon ending days later.

Self-Reminder Note for Carole…

EVERY DAY RISE AND GRAB PUSH BROOM TO SWEEP…ENDLESS CARRYING OUT PAILS OF DIRT AND DEBRIS TO GRASS AND SORT LATER

....

—

09 September

Morning meditation helps move ambitions to sweeping from sitting in lawn chair in pleasant early autumn sunshine. Warm winds and harvest season develop quiet mental lusts for relaxation and quiet. In distance prairie begins to sprout moving machinery. Trucks begin to pass by creating huge dust clouds. Activities of harvest ignite bruised feelings of loss and betrayal from family who seem to believe incapacity of thought without shame.

Push broom stands against wall of polka dot sunshine squares to wait for beginning of day. I like today's plan. Gather myself up from tent still standing in windy field but close to hedge sheltering out of worst.

When I first came here, "I will stay few days. I have tent to put up. What location seems best?" Carole said to land agent.

"Try close to hedge, over there," land agent said.

Now inside doors enough debris from doorway forms deposits in grass to left. Underneath debris of dirt and anything imaginable from one dead bird to broken boards still dangerous with nails small section of concrete foundation appears. Stunned now believe potential exists here in *Olde Homestead*.

Taking coffee break amuses my conscious enough to bring from car one chair thrown in with rest of tenting supplies. Lawn chair from accumulation of remains of apartment life with Alain now can sit on two foot by two feet concrete floor like slab in our suburban home's garage out of wind, rain and hot sun in doorway opening inside.

Finding useful garage ignites ambitions to keep on sweeping large area behind chair. Cook stove fuel, although getting low, boils water and enjoy cup of instant coffee. Powdered cream in coffee tops off the morning.

Sunshine with fresh air in front of doorway welcomes daily morning walk for exercise. Healthy choices like walking support decision to stay on without any prejudices towards *Olde Homestead.*

Bitterness wastes away with each step down grassy driveway towards gravel road. Large grain trucks begin to arrive creating thick dust billows, and must walk into deep ditch rampant with mosquitoes.

Each day bring out same clothes of growing layers of dirt and begin to clear room. The real use of this half room in square footage of total building evolving as hours add up. Having objectives each day to clear away foot high dust and dirt piles settles these new found ambitions of relocating to *Olde Homestead.*

Standing inside room realize the building evolves like combination shop and garage with dividing wall. Ladder of nailed pieces of three to four inch width foot and one half boards access attic area on shop side of wall where several items, even tattered brown suitcase sits.

I feel excitement of knowing the past of the haphazardness appearances of buildings in the middle of tall grasses becoming useful.

15 September

The end of the week seems like the most troubled Friday I've known. Banking issues resolve themselves where bank will pay back money I have paid, and news from government agency who process documents requires second trip to large city to figure out difficulties.

Relocation home project on *Olde Homestead* land seems to be developing more importance as a way of spending time, and valuing privacy for picturesque places.

Writing in journal:

Leaving past behind finds newness I experience as familiar. I am alone.

CHAPTER SEVEN

Dolorousness Crimes of Pasts

Before trip out to Nebraska and *Olde Homestead*, Carole returns to visit friends in another part downstate closer to border with Missouri and Nebraska. Karen, Yvette and Jessica, and Carole share in reunion information after many years of separate lives over lunch in rural area neighboring Nebraska. Karen became widow years back after tragic workplace accident with Billy. Nebraska restaurant provides comfortable air-conditioning retreat out of very hot weather. Karen, Yvette and Jessica listen without interrupting. Coffee ordered, Jessica likes tea, each order hot sandwiches and the meal Karen offers to pay for in celebration of their Reunion. Many years pass, and Carole shared some details earlier with Karen on phone about her recent trip to *Olde Homestead* in Nebraska.

As Karen chats with Yvette and Jessica said, "Where do you live now, Carole? Do you enjoy retirement, Jessica?

"Loving retirement, and live in suburbs nearby," Jessica said.

"Carole bought a farm in Nebraska," Karen said.

"Oh my god," Yvette said, and looks at photos Carole brings out as she shares updates of her own recent events.

"Two hundred thousand dollars is gone. Alain's health failed. But rent needs to be paid. Returning to Nebraska became an idea for alternative investment Alain and I discussed as our daily troubles began with Faith and Robert. The place requires much effort, and buildings remain on ten acres, but in need of windows and clearing."

"Oh my God twice as bad," Yvette said.

Carole said, "Somehow everything in Missouri fell apart for Alain and I and we often thought staying in Nebraska a better retirement alternative. After Alain passed away I receive a call from apartment building manager. Manager said Carole your rent has not been paid for six weeks, and we are deeply sorry. We all loved Alain and miss him. He was a grand man."

"So then I said my rent? Of course rent must be paid. Thank you. I guess Alain took care of this. I will get you a check as soon as possible I said. That very afternoon taking my vehicle to my local bank I pick up close friend, Sylvii, at home to accompany me. By this point I am feeling even worse and struggling with being alone. Faith seems to have gone on a trip to visit her own children. Sylvii, I met years back when we both become neighbors in suburbia, and always stay in touch.

Now as old friends living in new neighborhoods we often rely on the other one for support, help or sharing confidences."

"I really do not understand these events. Alain always had kept banking up-to-date, and careful with security keys. I wish I knew more."

"Earlier at my apartment Carole calling and I told Sylvii I called the bank financial adviser, Vivian. She seems to be vague and argumentative when I asked about my account and complaint about the problem with rent not being paid. Something's wrong Sylvii."

"In fact Sylvii said, Alain provided for you well, and loyal to you; Losing Alain seems like enough grief."

"I said, I am so grateful for the few days we have shared since the funeral Sylvii, and even staying over with you for nights alone now."

"After parking across in preferred parking lot for bank across their street, together we walk into our small but popular local bank. Tall blonde, well-dressed in suit female bank employer meets us in their bright waiting area of building we both know well from years of trying to make lifestyle choices like new cars and houses needing financing. Hello Carole, said Vivian. Everything seems fine at this point."

"Yet with my reply I introduce Sylvii with Vivian, dear friend Sylvii comes with me for our appointment. Will you agree to Sylvii sitting in on our meeting I said. Okay said Vivian and leading down short hallway past reach of row of tellers nearby. Vivian sits in large desk in bright corner office as sun streams through thin curtains with outside traffic noises close by. Vivian said your account cashed several checks to family members with whom Alain gave authority. Sylvii, here, also cashed one check."

"My devastation grows and turning with sideway stare I said, Sylvii, what happened? Friends help each other. Sylvii spoke up in our meeting, okay, Carole. I did receive a check but the money went into account to return money to you. I agreed to meeting with Faith and Robert last week at home after Alain passed away. Robert called on telephone and asked to speak to me about their father and said we want to compensate you for your loyalty to Dad. Robert and Faith came next day and met at my home. I was so confused but curious. I, of course felt confusion at this odd development, and said to Robert are you sure of your ability to write me a check? Syllvii said she did not understand either and felt such extreme anxiety of the meeting and their visit. She said she cashed the check to keep money for me so she took their check. I try to stay composed after knowing Sylvii well these years."

Vivian sits listening and staring at Sylvii. Three women sit in sunny corner office discussing my financial losses as if normal. Vivian said with Alain's deteriorating health, Alain's children claimed their Power of Attorney said bank employee, Vivian. My world and everything fell apart in these moments," Carole said.

Karen, Yvette and Jessica listen as sitting across and next from Carole at the table. Yvette said, "Your children took all your money Carole? What about police? Do they help you?"

"We reported everything later same day. At the bank I assure Vivian this transaction wrong. We have a joint account, and we benefit each other. Vivian continues with saying the bank safety deposit box was broken by Robert. You must pay to fix the damage said Vivian. I should not have to pay anything I told her. Alain keeps keys like safety boxes on our night stand in small container. What about all my funds I said."

"Vivian quips with you can still use the account and government checks will continue to be deposited and Alain's pension checks, bank person Vivian said. What about the police? Sylvii said. Did you call the police? No, Vivian said. The bank estimates this as family issue not criminal activity effecting bank. I know Alain and Carole these wonderful couple benefit each other in event of loss. I am close to them both, Sylvii said."

'Experience of financial losses over Alain's death and my wealth become very frightening I tell police. The bank employer stares at Sylvii. That's up to you Carole to report to police said bank employee, Vivian, confirms bank did not call the police. Criminal matters are your's to deal with if crimes committed here.'

"To support each other if something happens to me then Alain benefits, if something happens to Alain then I benefit," I said to Vivan. We trusted bank to look after our money. How can this happen? I expect to pay rent as Alain and I have paid rent with Alain alive and well. Finally Vivian admits my children,

Faith and Robert said the government will look after you." "Though, our meeting continued, this must be wrong said Sylvii. Vivian said can you have your doctor complete this form? Vivian hands over her desk her bank's one page form and said Carole, Can you ask your doctor to complete bank form and return to our bank?"

"For instance, can I help? said Sylvii. I can hold onto form, and taking form from Vivian Sylvii said, Let's go see your doctor after we leave here. He may be able to assist us. I took the bank form, but handing to Sylvii said, okay to visiting my doctor right away, and with Sylvii left bank, walk through lobby and to car across street in lot from bank. I said to Sylvii, please drive. After handing over the car keys, Sylvii said we'll go to see your doctor in office down next Street."

"We drive few blocks from bank and go in to doctor's office. Can we see Doctor today for emergency development? After waiting few minutes in nearby empty waiting room, but soon receptionist leads us into doctor's office."

"Doctor, I said, we come from bank and banking representative gave this form as I need to deal with Alain's passing and our financial interests like paying my rent. Bank employee gave us her banking form to complete by my doctor. Our children, Faith and Robert used Alain's Power of Attorney and took all our investment funds. How can this happen?"

"Sylvii said I knew nothing of problems, Doctor, but I was with Carole at the bank a few moments ago. We have only come from the bank now, where bank told us their children, Robert and Faith withdrew our funds from Alain's joint account to drain Carole's and Alain's account of investment funds. I said bank explains issue as Robert and Faith using Alain's Power of Attorney. Doctor leans against table across his small examination room and nearby. They did not have permission, Doctor, to take our money. I knew nothing of this. No, I am not filling this form out for bank Doctor said. Sylvii took the form and said we will go now.

We walk out into Doctor's quiet sunny parking lot, Sylvii said, I can drive you home Carole." "Furthermore as we enter apartment, we pass not speaking to building manager, and take elevator up to Carole's and and Alain's fourth floor large apartment. We sit in my small sitting room and I said to Sylvii, 'We must call the police. Okay, Sylvii said.'"

"On the phone in my apartment and nearby, Sylvii makes the call. I need to report a theft. Soon officer taking call said, can I have the details mam? Sylvii said I am Carole's good friend and now sitting with dear friend. We have been to bank. Friend just lost her husband, Alain. His wife must pay her rent, so no rent being paid we went to bank to ask of details. That's when bank staff member told us my friend Carole's children drain all cash from her joint investment account with her husband, Alain, and use their power of attorney."

"I took phone from Sylvii and said I went to the bank, found my money taken, and children withdrew all our investment money. This situation must be wrong or bank error. Can you look into these details? Officer Wilkins said I can forward your complaint to prosecutor's office to investgate, and request to follow-through. Thanks said Sylvii. Then Sylvii said it's done, Carole, and you have done the best and right thing."

"How can this happen Jessica? These are our children, my children. Alain never would have done this," Carole said.

"We went back to my bank again next day. Sylvii said Carole, please walk to teller. I'm beside you said Sylvii. Teller stands across cubicle in row of teller posts of banks. I said, I'm closing my account. Teller said, 'Buying new car?'

'No, I said. Teller looks up my bank account.'

'One thousand, five hundred dollars in account to write bank draft. Fine, I said.'

"Teller hands over bank draft closing account. Sylvii said thank you. We walk out of the bank to Sylvii's vehicle, and Syvli said now we will go to my bank on other side of city. Okay I said. Banking business across town seemed quiet in one warm autumn afternoon offering seating to waiting customers in lobby. Let's sit here Carole, said Sylvii. Wait until we find manager to help," Carole said.

Sylvii walks over to teller to request manager, and returns to sit with Carole.

'Hello, Sylvii,' said manager, male in mid forties. 'Lucky to find me here on such a brilliant autumn day. Let's go into my office.'

We follow into small office nearby.

—

'I am helping Carole cope with some troubling developments at her bank. Carole closed her account, and my personal attorney suggests we set up joint account, like with me and as now Carole's husband, Alain, has passed on two months ago. Carole found out her children Faith and Robert drain her's and Alain's life savings after we visit her bank to settle up papers for Carole's widow benefits claims. Carole told me to call local police, and Carole made the complaint official to police, Sylviii said.'

'Yes manager said. The bank supports this move Sylvii. Joint accounts between friends although not common bank cooperates with….Manager draws out banking agreement and we both, Carole and Sylvii, sign. Okay. Looks fine we both agree.'

'I am afraid we will have even more trouble said Sylvii. Neither of Carole's children, Robert or Faith have shown any indication of correcting their use and theft of Carole's assets and before their father's death. Can you protect Carole? Carole requires all of her widow benefits from her husband's widow benefits to pay rent. Some funds left help pay for small personal care like hair dressers said Sylvii. The bank puts red flags on accounts like this to warn employees to any odd or aggressive actions taken on account said Manager. Carole can deposit the bank draft from her bank to account today, and then pay her rent said Sylvii.'

'All of this develops yesterday morning at bank. We have been to Carole's doctor refusing to cooperate over any disadvantage in Carole's health, my lawyer, Mr.

George telling me to help Carole close bank and open new bank account, and we make complaint to local police. I cancel the power of attorney Faith and Robert have over my health. I believe we do enough but with Faith and Robert, you never know said Sylvii.'

Next afternoon I call Sylvii on telephone. Sylvii, I shared cup of coffee with neighbor in lounge area this morning. Of course neighbor said I must avoid conversations with Faith or Robert and she was so kind to suggest I set up post-dated automatic cheques to pay rent. Will you drop by later today or tomorrow to stop in at building manager's office to set up this arrangement? Yes, of course said Sylvii. Carole, I am proud to be your friend and help and great news for support from speaking to neighbors I wish makes great deal of difference I hope for your sense of feeling safe in your apartment building.

That afternoon Sylvii drops by my apartment. Sylvii said Carole you have come up with wonderful solution to writing checks each month. Let's go speak to building manager. Thanks Sylvii. I am hopeful to look after some of my business now without Alain.

Downstairs after getting off elevator on main floor down hallway building manager's office doorway opens exposing Rhea working at her desk. Sylvii knocking said Rhea, do you have a few moments? Of course said Rhea, and I said I have been speaking to neighbor, another tenant yesterday who suggests automatic payments with void check as easy solution. Sylvii brought out one of our new checks to our new joint account, now a joint account with Sylvii set up at Sylvii's bank after closing all accounts at our bank where Alain had done business. Sylvii helps me with business during this time.

Okay. Rhea said, and accepted void cheque Sylvii offers across manager's desk.

Will my rent be paid now each month?

Yes, said Rhea. Your account on this cheque will deduct rent each month back in May 1993.

Carole goes on with description of recent times during lunch with Karen, Yvette and Jessica.

"Later after going up the elevator back to Carole's apartment, 'Sylvii said, Sunday is Mother's Day. Can I pick you up for Mass at ten in the morning. There will be short tea after services at the Church, and then I thought together a stop off at our local Gerome Park, time to reflect together and enjoy some nature? Right. Let's go. Mother's Days seem like a struggle after losing Gabriel to distances for his education but I want to remember how Gabriel helped me feel like his valuable Mom with his day to day good nature said Sylvii. Shall we go to Mass again next week or week after? I enjoy going so much but the drive may be too long I think, Carole said.

I think you have great thoughts and suggestions Carole. I will love to pick you up for Mass. *Carole continues description to Yvette, Karen and Jessica* Next Sunday in May...

Sylvii walking into Carole's apartment building sees the concierge in front and said I am picking up Carole for Sunday Mass. Carole waits and sits in back loung area said Jane. Sylvii smiles her thank you and wanders through to main floor lounge.

Oh I am sorry Carole. I did not expect to see you visiting with Robert and Cheryl I thought we were going to Sundary Mass. *ha ha*, can you imagine?

We can leave now, Cheryl said. I think going Mass so great. Robert stood quietly behind the sitting Cheryl saying no welcoming words to me or even Sylvii after she arrived. Cheryl got up and walks out of lounge with Robert. Are you fine Carole? said Sylvii. I am so glad you came this morning Sylvii I said. What a relief.

Next day I call Sylvii. Sylvii, I am going to call police again. Weeks and now months seem to pass and no action. Will you come sit with me while I make the call and guide me through the results. I have been wondering the very same things said Sylvii. I will tell Wallace I am going out to see you, and I can be right over in twenty minutes.

We drop in to apartment manager's office with check. Manager said everything fine now, and rent will automatically paid out of this new account between Sylvii and you, Carole. Upstairs in apartment Sylvii and Carole relax before lunch.

Okay. What about police? Let us call again to officer Wilkins? On business card Officer Wilkins left number to call Sylvii said. Officer Wilkins soon answers. Hello, this is Carole, Alain's wife. Have you got news of our theft of Alain's and my account from children. Yes Carole. The prosecutor's office investigate these matters Officer Wilkins said. What can a woman do? I am leaving the state for another job across the country Office Wilkins said. Sylvii took the receiver from Carole to listen to call. Carole gives me receiver Officer Wilkins to speak to Sylvii.

'Thanks mam. We believe your verbal statements helpful to explain these details and ask if Carole able to provide written statement said Officer Wilkins.' Sylvii puts down receiver to say Officer Wilkins transfers to another state but another officer will be in touch and to send my complaint to State Attorney's office. He asked for me to complete formal statement and will come here next week on Tuesday.

Next week Officer MacWilliam, second state police officer to investigate, arrives at my apartment.

Officer said to Sylvii waiting wth me in my apartment, can we have privacy, mam? Officer MacWilliam asks for privacy from Sylvii. Can you wait downstairs while we speak Sylvii I said to Sylvii.

Sylvii said I'll wait in lobby.

My statement went like this:

'I went to the bank, found my money taken, and children taken all money. This situation must be wrong or bank error. Can you look into these details?' I told Officer MacWilliam everything.

Four thousand dollars remains available and amount of check Alain's children gave to Sylvii.

'I think we must call the police or state prosecutor's office again. I'm afraid said Carole. Yes, I agree said Sylvii. The bank duty is to you for your trust to look after Alain and you, Carole, and your shared money said Sylvii.'

Yvette, Karen, Yvette and Jessica say little over their reunion with old friend, Carole. Each listens and I am grateful for their closeness of old friends, and listening. Too much happens. Their own lives seem to evolve with successes in business in Nebraska. Each have families nearby but nothing happens like happens to Carole. The *Olde Homestead* sounds like great challenge beyond their own imaginations.

Are Sylvii and I just very good and better friends. These friends say little or offer to do nothing to contribute to any resolution. No offers of help; sort of mocking tones I am not able to comprehend. Why not help reporting such serious events in anyone's life? Why not help me? Or am I not remaining one of their chosen few?

Chapter Eight

Relocating

19 September 1994

I left Sagebrush Monday 11 September for visit with old friend. Last visit many years ago values closeness even with not seeing for many many years. I sleep overnight in home of old friend. Next day depart for return to home-location, and develop plan to travel to large city hours away for more information and resolution of visa issues to Thailand.

Tuesday September at six thirty in afternoon
18 September

    Carole writes in her journal.
    Writing about first roadtrip to Sagebrush in August

Coming Home July 1984

Next Year Returning Home in July

—

Writing some notes helps to ease spirits or hopes for returning home when my own advice suggests alternative directions.

So I left but alone walking home too at 6:30 pm

Years earlier Sunday

My flight lands in afternoon but 4:30 pm. The plane lands late from Thailand and from Europe to this large city.

I'm invited to lunch, and we go to fastfood joint. One close pal must return to his home, and leaves for bus, train and boat.

Invitations to visit are welcoming until Friday, then will drive alone to home.

1994 July
Carole writes in evening at 7:30 pm Thursday August 2nd

Sylvii describes plan for arranging relocations with Carole to Fern in their lunch together in Fern's home in nearby suburbs, and away from Carole's apartment. Sylvii refused invitation from Carole's grandson, dear Randy to attend their birthday party gathering at Carole's apartment earlier in week so is making up the event with lunch and cake with dear old pals Fern, who invites church friend, Iris.

Sitting nearby Sylvii said, "Next year's holiday decisions must include Carole's choice to go to Sagebrush, you old dears."

"Of course. I know Carole struggles with adjustments too. I admire how you have been supportive of Carole with police and banking people. Carole lost alot. I'm sorry but but Carole's banking losses known to others bring clarity to myself. I lost huge amounts from husband and bank associate using both names to invest and lost all. What I can do? Seems like police do nothing, or I am a fool alone as no one listens to these kind of complaints like husband and wife stuff," Iris said.

NEXT YEAR'S DECISION
Lunch with friends eases choice to return to *Olde Homestead.*
02 August

Next day quiet location puts distances between past now filling with renewals after years of absences. Bird twitters everywhere, mostly south treeline. Car trip shortens trip today with stops for reunions with dear old friends, Yvette, Karen and Jessica and arrive at 2:30 in great shape *at Olde Homestead* with packed lunch from dear old Karen invigorating my spirits. I begin to enjoy sunshine in tall grasses and distances with fields like checkerboards. Staying around Karen and Yvette or even Jessica I believe will encourage great things and new supports after troubles with finding Robert and Faith out of their thefts of Alain's and my savings.

Putting up tent in field takes tons of time and with collapsing but three hours later after restoring my confidences with quiet to myself affirmations, like you can do this Carole, and building up with completing tent assembly. Taking my time am deciding to walk with briefness of sounds of birds or sites of deer or foxes nearby and carry two objects resembling sticks like weights and wear travel suitcase I carry like a backpack.

Details of furthering investigations.

Next year.
Wandering Ways
Homestead Acreage at Sagebrush 03 August

Recent visits with old friends in upstate Nebraska and great weather to sit outside; and we took drive past State University, main streets and old apartment habitats. Left next day, and arrive with new hopes of changes for consequences of Alain's illness and passing bringing me here. Next day in leaving visits with old friends for quiet location distances close between past of true friends instead of ghosts after events in the bank and back in Missouri.

Bird twitters everywhere, mostly south treeline. Car trip shortens with reunions nearby to arrive at 2:30 in afternoon at *Olde Homestead*. Lunch from with dear old friends Karen, Yvette and Jessica invigorating my spirits, Begin to enjoy sunshine in tall grasses and distances with fields like checkerboard. Putting up tent in field takes tons of time, and collapsing but three hours later tent assembly looks fine enough to finish, walk with weights and backpack over quiet country road.

Day 1: Last night's thunder and lightning rain storm started at 1 a.m. lasting until 2:30 a.m. but tent pegs held and I stay dry. The bottom of the sleeping bag got wet as it was placed along the left wall from door. The puddles of water near the door were downslope so did not bother me. The wind was strong knocking over the small water jug but all the tent pegs held the tent and the tent fly stayed on top outside of tent. I placed the tent about fifteen feet from the caraganna hedge and north grove of poplar trees with the hedge holding back the wind. Outside, new five gallon compost pail toilet and lid were placed in front of caraganna hedge still standing and with few disturbances by wind or rain storm. Reusable but new-to-me styrofoam from packing become my seating accommodations, and did not blow away but the bag of old gloves find soaked. Everything else remains dry inside the car.

Breakfast and dressing in my acreage clothes is an effort. I feel like I want to be very lazy like the old days in the cabin with family. The sadness from my family's losses at bank days and weeks before staying with me. My newly acquired old friends shakes me into new times and relationships left behind decades before...

As told to Yvette, Jessic and Karen

'I have lost all my money to them,' Carole had said to Yvette, Jessica and Karen.

'What kind of conditions occur? they said.'

'After Alain passed, I went to bank for advice with Carole on advice for absent rent cheque and paying Carole's apartment fees. Financial adviser, Vivian told Carole her daughter and son, had used a power of attorney Alain wrote to drain their account.'

We eat lunch, but Carole said, "Letting you know I have plans to depart very soon for France or Thailand. I am happier elsewhere. I found place hours away to redo up to being short term home when in country again. Nothing left but bunches of memories now sitting in losses of this sort of theft I know nothing about. Alain left lots of help for me but not this. He never lost his love and I for him…'

'Nebraska offers many changes and Missouri apartment sits idle, Carole said.'

'We've been old friends. We had no idea. Horrible, said Karen.'

"With money losses at bank," Carole said, "Anger and shock remain very real, and I struggle with finding alternatives through police, friends and agencies. Staying local and dormant risks even more. I am afraid for myself."

Next day drive to *Olde Homestead* near Sagebrush, Nebraska.

August 1995

Now, far away in sunshine and rustling trees invite higher spirits for trying. Pulling purple thistle today is made easy by heavy rains at 7:30 pm.

Saturday, Days 02 to 04 August

—

Light rain last night and today with mosquitos thick and nasty. After a cold breakfast of bread with fruit sauce, I put on my boots to walk to the storage, granary I call my sylo. I am relieved the interior seems clean with floor swept leaving plywood undisturbed. Last time new lock remains in place on exterior small short door. I must crouch over to reach in. My push broom lays on the floor in front of me as left. Twenty dollars bought the black and decker broom laying inside front door of sylo I purchase last summer from local hardware with gas station. My Coleman burner stove sits to the right of the door unharmed. The box seems damp but when removed to outdoors, seems fine. I'll take the stove back for storage with me because anxieties of any loss like small stove wrecks feelings for well-being. The long walk to the sylo from tool shop ends over but successful. I brought own shovel in car last time lays beside push broom as left.

Grateful, I take the partial used propane canister from car trunk. Start-up the propane to light the stove and heat my water for a cup of coffee. I bring my coffee into the sunshine and lay on the grass, doing nothing. Light rains start. Then I put on my boots to clean up some animal mess left – I'm not sure what – the mess is large pieces and a dead bird. I've begun to assemble tool shop items to photograph to try to sell to antique dealer.

So today I remember my backpack for the hour walk plus twenty minutes earlier. Supper develops with biscuits and sauce with half bottle water. No sunset from roaming clouds. I saw a helicopter this afternoon, low flying west at 7:30 pm.

Sunday, Days 03...05 August

Rest and relaxation seem relevant today. Quieting myself from the anxiety of the unknown or being alone is met with yellow warblers high upon the power line disconnected to the tool shop. I look at the old barn and realize I want it to be reused so I will add these photos too to review with local vintage store in the hopes of a sale. I wash my hair and sun myself. Black tea for breakfast pleasant with bread and oatmeal. My food seems to be lasting the week. I pruned the driveway caraganna with the small axe and am pleased in my confidence. I've been doubting my decision not to return to Thailand then realize due to the experiences I had last year with my passport it was a good idea to hold out for more money. Going to Paris to work may be a future opportunity but I am trying to convince them the cost to travel not reasonable. I put a bright green plastic strap on the door to tool shop from packing from shipping container from Thailand.

So tomorrow I will photograph as much as possible....getting the oil can off the shelf is the biggest problem. Two tuna sandwiches for supper is extravagant as I used one can. It's odd how this simple existence too becomes closer to my old life.

Thursday August

—

Wednesday drove to Library to and with visit to Tax Assessment Office. Fifty-Two Dollars for agricultural taxes by check; Take local copy of rural map; signed petition for Rural Funds.

Took walk down mainstreet. Coffee Shop looks spiffy with new frontage upgrade. Small town mural designs across street are very attractive with concrete flower pots and petunias new steel benches for resting. Librarian asks advice about holidaying. I suggested nice spots in Missouri. The general store appears busy and did have many customers.

Thirty dollars – but not propane. Gas station had no propane cylinders...Two dollars for one gallon of gasoline for car. I took a different road to town – twelve miles past the red buildings – left from my driveway – returned same way.

Cooked two porkchops, whole onion, cabbage – coleslaw. Big meal. Walked six times down driveway at noon.

Saturday 11 August

Friday becomes my disaster. Thursday afternoon I smear soap over my face as an insect/mosquito repellant which burnt my face and inflamed red-eye. I took it easy all day – barely eating not cooking. Saturday was better; I opened the sleeping bag and slept as if in a bed. A sleeping bag is not very comfortable and is confining. There was a frightening windstorm in the night. The wind came out of silence and was like an ocean and very noisy. The tent is holding together well. Saturday morning I ate a banana and bun with juice and left for the market in….However, clerk at hardware store says it will be Thursday. So I hope I will plan well and return Thursday. The grass was cut in front of the property late this afternoon – but only the grass bordering the driveway exposing the entrance.

Today I took some pictures at beach from the shoreline. Robert's birthday tomorrow –

Tuesday, 14 August

Monday is cloudy. I need a rest. The water almost gone. After a piece of bread, a hotdog bun and banana and vitamins, I drove to gas station and asked for water. They filled my five gallon water tank and small container for free at the garage. After I drove down main street to the Return Depot but it is open 12 – 12:30 Tuesday to Friday.

Five Dollars for lunch at Coffee Shop sitting on main street nearby, and I enjoy soup and sandwich and coffee and chat with owner about life in small town Nebraska.

Later I drove around to local, small motel for the information in event I decide on to visit if tent collapses.

First thing this morning I bought groceries at food market, and probably last remainder of trip to *Olde Homestead.*

Thirty-two dollars and bug spray. Mosquitoes are bad.

Wednesday, 15 August

The day stays very quiet. No harvest nearby. Smoke from northern fires is back but mosquitoes and black flies continue. Off spray is helping reduce the size of the bites. I moved breakfast location to behind the car and I rest against the trunk's bumper. I took my coffee and lawn chair to cleared activity area I now call the Garage. My plan to climb the wall ladder changes. I knocked down the linoleum ceiling in shop with a pole instead. I continued shoveling and moving tool boxes until three in afternoon. I took lunch break at two o'clock. Tuna on hotdog buns and peach fit my hunger needs. Taking a nap in the car late in afternoon becoming regular and treat to me for relaxation. Local smoke from forest fire and mosquitoes are too thick to walk in. Getting a bit more rest seems okay. The Alanon book, "How Alanon Works" is helping. Many from my old home group in Missouri have passed on. I still believe meetings are the best blessings for those lost to disease.

Friday, 17 August

The heavy dew seems less. Breakfast in sunshine is comfortable but I now can take my lawn chair and instant coffee to the garage to sit inside away from mosquitoes. A few bees fly by.

I think the wire and nails continue to be a hazard. Washing some underwear in a basin and sunshine almost normal as I witness in Thailand. I don't have to deal with student or walkers as was situation… experience is revealing to me. How I judge and judge myself is not objective but subjective?

I drive to local Walmart at 10:30. Store bathroom looks clean, and look at travel suitcases for enjoyment. I am stunned by the amount of traffic. McDonald's restaurant sits nearby where we spent Robert's birthday, his fourth birthday with sparklers. The market begins at 4 pm. I drove to downtown streets, park, walk a bit and found city library. They will let me tutor adhoc Monday, Tuesday evenings next spring, summer. So I've completed the logistics. Two hours per week English as Second Language lessons are possible while in Sagebrush, and left for vegetable market at 4 pm. It's nice, easy to find, few stalls, and I receive the information to call for tables to rent. I bought bee honey lip and skin balm in lemon grass for mosquitoes from farmer and two cobs of corn. Seven in evening.

Sunday, 19 August
August, Wednesday at 10:00 am
Bird Watching I

Bright, completely yellow small bird perched on purple flowering thistle blossoms. Siting is less than five minutes in large field but in front and near the caraganna hedge beside well… "drinking instant coffee in vintage garage; sitting on a lawn chair."

"canary" perching across the driveway approximately one hundred feet directly in front of my chair.

August Saturday at 11:00 am.

While preparing my breakfast, a yellow midsize bird sast perched on an old dismantled powerline between Barn and pole beside Well. The bird fluffed his wings to expose black on the underside The singing lasted at minimum five minutes, warbling. Same bird flew directly west, slightly north in cuve towards the corner large poplar trees of property frontage. No similar birds flocked. Unsure if bird title warbler?

20 August Barn

A few pails of straw and dirt easily clear the stalls. Sweeping will tidy the stalls enough to move the contents of toolshop. The barn is ideal for wreath-making if ever.

Second removal of moss from two of three vintage shop doors clears the bottom of Right-Door. There is an opening and daylight to shop. The Left-Door is in better shape but grass problem is serious. 7:30 pm

Tuesday, 21 August

Slept until 08:30 am alarm. Cold at middle of night is hard on sleeping. Long breakfast until 11:30 am. Left for Returns-Depot...

One dollar net from drink bottles with few picked-up tins along gravel road in front. Staff provide great service. Filled five gallon water at Sagebrush Gas Station before going to Public Library.

Atmosphere is homey-like welcoming, and fit in nice long visit. Shopped at Sagebrush's grocery. Big supper of porkchop, coleslaw and cauliflower.

Take walk in evening as common practice.

7 pm
Wednesday, August; Thursday, August

A new sketch for Yellow Autumn Leaves in the am. help me to feel grateful to new discovery wild buffalo bean flower patch beside new path to barn.

I weed out thistle to discover the number of flowers increasing. Removing all the wild dandelion is next.

Sweeping barn stalls is complete on left for storage of vintage machinery pieces and from shop across mid acre of ten acres.

Thursday, 23 August

One in morning…early this morning I woke; I found the letter with recruiter's messages from Thailand in notes in my packing and requests my registration with teaching in more conservative approach. ie. teaches youngsters as age five years is youngest student. Next morning I complete form for request for scheduling. My self-introduction is next by telephone at public library.

"Hello, my name is Carole. In July, I return to Thailand and a country city after years ago completing two years of teaching English as a Foreign Language teacher at the Thailand College and students sixteen to twenty-two years of age.

During my summer vacation, I travel to Sagebrush USA, and relax and work to restore and refurbish ten acres and buildings where Europeon immigrants began their home decades or some years ago. While relaxing I enjoy watercolour painting, sketching with a lead pencil on reusable envelopes from which I've already received my personal mail. I've been on my acreage three to four weeks and in four weeks will travel by car four hours back to Missouri.

Friday, 24 August

The weather is cold and windy. I ate one banana sandwich, cookies and a juice box for breakfast before leaving and Timmies for coffee in a restaurant. The Public Library opens at 12:30. They are welcoming, and to my work, even upstairs for next three hours to complete the applications.

Sunday, 26 August

For Saturday 25 August heavy rain in the night created a very wet ground making weed and grass pulling extreme but easier. The tool shop front is clear within six feet but low grass exists. I started the West Side with thick dark grass and lifted the grass previously walked on. Last year's grass causes a problem of ground sticking and even rodent holes so carry pulled grass

—

to a compost location. Sorting contents of shop takes hours and in removable salvage if possible. Two boxes, one with glass, one with vintage oiling tools will be removed, clean and, for possible sale. The remaining contents will be stored in Barn. 13:23 hours

Believing in the shortened pace of the final stage of storing contents in barn helps decide to gather all grass and weed clippings to one central location, where the car was parked and grass trampled. The two piles of dirt from *Olde Homestead's* garage sit nearby but very close to cooking location. Debris of dirt and insulation wood shavings shoveling and moving to a new location across the main driveway. I had been cooking next to this very contaminated-looking soil. These two tasks took three hours. The sunset can be seen and sets at seven forty-five in evening.

Monday, 27 August

Shopped in town for supplies and food. Stop into library later. Car repairs go well at local garage and time spent to repair car radiator before leaving town allows for walk around area. Receptionist suggests staying away from area in front of bank due to vagrants bothering others. One quick stop at grocery mart finds and buys sausage for tonight's meal. Bought Sausage! 7:30 pm

CHAPTER NINE

Natural Events

Natural consequences bring results to value *Olde Homestead's* location with resources including new relationships with local habitat.

Tuesday, 28 August
Bird Watching II

1. 11:30 Flock of the small yellow birds, I think are warblers or so been told, visit caragana hedge across driveway beside well pump. Wax-wing name out of caragana on corner of wellhouse to perch.
2. 12:00 All flew diagonal south or one yellow flew west. They all disappeared by 12:00 noon. Warbler is covered in most-bright-yellow with small-grey spot; Waxwing is red-grey colour with black head and brim-like-hat;

Wednesday, 29 August

Much warmer last night. The tent was comfortable. Left for Garage and oil change at 10:00 am but found out the car requires motor work.

One hundred dollars for new motor thermometer and reminding me how poor and too foolish or not able to afford to drive for a job appointment. Maybe I can work a deal for costs; go to Paris; go to London.

Thursday, 30 August

For third day this week, I drive to Diamond City to complete car repair. As repair took 90 minutes, I took a walk to the nearby local Mission, and ask to meet the Pastor and tour. I asked if I could stay for lunch and, "Yes," he said, "Soup and sandwich."

Pastor remains sole manager andone service a week on Sunday but he was interested in my past and paying work in English as Foreign Language in Thailand and work history. I told him of my acreage nearby, and hope he visits in the future. The car repair seems a success. 7 pm.

Friday, 31 August,
Bird Watching III
Four-forty-five in afternoon.

One yellow bird with grey chest, maybe a warbler, flew alone to carragannas. Last evening was warm and same birds were perching lower in carraganna hedge beside decompost five gallon pail fifteen feet from tent.

The front lawn is emptying as I sort to store in barn. The ceiling linoleum is planned as tent pad in garage for next visit. The wind is strong and has blown tent fly off yesterday and today. The row of north poplars is turning gradual shades of yellow. While moving and digging with shovel, moss from the north side of toolshop, I found the concrete lip to foundation that would have been the carpenter's from Homestead efforts to seal the base. I'm planning to create a six foot wide grass free perimeter around toolshop.

Sunday, 02 September

Saturday, I attend Diamond City Farmers Market. Weather feels cold with rain, only ten stalls with vegetable, teas, soaps, deodorants. T-shirts fit in, - wonder about cost to attend? I did not talk to anyone. Heavy rain in afternoon causes temperature to drop, very cold last night. I'm completing moving toolshop contents to barn from lawn, - but shop still needs clearing. Maybe I'll finish. Last night at 10:15 brilliant sky filled with stars and Milky Way above horizon to horizon.

Reference: 01 September, from Beach Labor Day Sunday One in afternoon I'm eating lunch at beach picnic tables, tuna sandwiches. I'll take a walk down the beach, take photos of colours, and streets. Windy and warm weather encouraged me. 1 pm.

Neighbor's husband, describes farm parts as, "One-hundred year old parts."

Monday, 03 September

While at Diamond City bought used door for shop for few dollars from rummage sale. Customers and owner alike ask about *Olde Homestead*, and welcome them to tour the acreage; They may look at contents. Later in day one rummage seller arrives with her friend and did not ask or take anything; nice to visit couple hours from two to four in afternoon, and left at five. Very sunny today.

Bird Watching IV

No birds in morning; No birds at 11:00 am.

Rain began overnight – staying wet all day. Turning left at driveway is the easier drive this year to Sagebrush gas station provides free water.

Fifty cent hotdogs in gas station fast food spot. I bought hot dog with water for lunch; used garage bathroom, bought gasoline; third fill-up at gas station equals four fill-ups of gasoline equals quantities of amount of gasoline to drive to acreage. Sitting in warm car passes afternoon.

Tuesday, 04 September

Last night temperature went to zero degress but frost is not obvious. Very cold and hard to sleep. I went to Sagebrush Library. Weather is to warm to seventy degrees tomorrow with lows to forty-five degrees.

—

The garage is colder so I'm convinced not any longer I can put the tent inside. I should finish up soon and prepare to leave on the Tuesday,

18 September. 7 pm.

Reference: Sun has almost set in twenty minutes.

Wednesday, 05 September

Getting up at 6 am, I saw frost on the tent zipper flap and walked out into a layer of frost on everything, even the car. I slept off and on with strange nightmares with my Dad. I felt a bit jumpy and thought the very large bumble bee was inside the tent but bee sitting on the tent wall outside in morning sunshine. The sky was blue with first slice of a new moon in the east. First thing is to wash underwear.

2. Soak feet in used water;

3. clean toenails;

4. wash car with used water;

5. wash hair; put basin on hood with two cups cold water; shampoo twice and condition.

The sun shone with much warmth so I made a huge lunch. I used dirty water to take road dirt off car and bugs.

One fried pork chop, corn on cob, four potatoes, two slices of Italian bread with coleslaw are cooked, eaten and hair dries all sitting in warm sunshine. At 3 pm. I have to begin chores. Next day in my phone all to register with Reserve Unit in Peace Corps, like Mrs. Lilian Carter, clerk declined my application due to sixty years compulsory maximum age and training schedules.

Today, I walked up to metal round sylo granary to replace items I had photographed when I arrived. Seems to take three hours but there weren't many to put away. The 7-Up bottle removed from rummage from toolshop taken for deposit which has gone well in Sagebrush. I haul large items from front yard to barn; long sharp triangle shape steel part; longboard, long metal narrow panel. As I do self-maintenance most of the day I decide not to sit in sun to finish the watercolor; 6:45 pm.

Thursday, 06 September

Emptying decomposable toilet is heavy work but without this toilet, these four weeks would not be possible. 7 pm.

Friday, 07 September

Heavy windstorm collapses the tent. The wind is from east and no tree barrier. Starting at 10 pm. lasting until 09:00 am., I had to leave the collapsing tent at 07:30 am. I wore my pj's for first time to car, (or maybe second) and changed to make oatmeal bread, orange and coffee. There was a very wide streak of lightning across the north sky, thunder and heavy downpour from 09:30 to 11:00 am. I changed clothes, jeans, sweater.

—

Chapter Ten

Saturday Night

Back in Missouri and visiting, Carole on Saturday, becomes like a ritual to Sylvii as often weekends seem particularly sad or lonely and when families often gather for meals together. "I'll make some tea Carole," said Sylvii. "How have things been? I made some inquiries about returning to France.

"I wish to go alone, Sylvii," said Carole. "You know Faith and Robert drop by too often and keep reminding me I must cooperate with moving to government run facility.

"Are you afraid of them Carole? How long has this been happening?"

"Awhile now. Sometimes I think of them creeping in when asleep as Faith still has apartment key."

"Call 911 Carole," said Sylvii. "Your phone sits on table here."

At that moment cleaning staff knock on door and Carole said, "Come in""Checking on you this evening to ask if your in need of laundry services or personal care services," said cleaning and maid services.

"Well we have to look for your passport, see your passport if current or order you a new issue," Sylvii said.

"I am so weak with grief. But okay. I hope the Missouri ID card we renewed together to be enough. A new passport application seems next step after mine went missing from safety deposit box."

"I go out the back way Carole. Front door locks at ten o'clock. It's just past ten now." "We'll talk next week after I obtain some application forms to apply for my new passport," Carole said.

Next day, as Sylvii drove to early morning mass her car was side swiped and left incapacitated in hospital for weeks. Good byes with not seeing Carole takes months As Sylvii lay at home often with broken legs healing her spouse, Wallace did all housework, yardwork and errands for groceries or prescriptions.

"Sylvii said. "I called Carole, and she will drop by today for afternoon tea and cakes. Do you want to join us Wallace?"

"Yes, I think I want to share support with you for helping Carole, Sylvii. I know she has been through tough times with losing Alain. Did you get it all sorted with police and Faith and Robert?" Wallace said.

"I am not sure," said Sylvii. "When we spoke on telephone Carole agreed to visiting today but nothing else."

"I can help too you know; You are laid up very badly with two broken legs and lucky that's all," Wallace said.

"Okay," said Sylvii. "I agree with you on that. Doctor said I won't be without leg supports for many months and walking with crutches best choice to stay active. I am beginning to feel more like my old self after shock of accident though," Sylvii said.

"That's the doorbell," Wallace said, "so I will go welcome Carole I hope."

"Carole," Wallace said. "We both wait and so delighted to see you today. Sylvii invited me to join you two for tea."

"Oh," said Carole. "I am glad to see you but things are kind of tough these days you know since Alain passed away. Faith and Robert, my two grown children, stole all my money."

"Come," Wallace said. "Let us sit with Sylvii. She is in breakfast room on sofa couch we brought in. She is still very laid up with two broken legs."

Sylvii said, "Oh, Carole, what a great relief to see you today. My legs resting here on sofa are broken from car accident so many weeks ago."

"I am happy to see you but things have been very bad Sylvii, and I have some very bad news."

Wallace brought china tea pot to table with three cups and saucers. "Can I pour the tea Sylvii?"

"Thanks " said Sylvii. "Carole, I told Wallace our details about events at the bank last autumn. Have police been in touch?"

"No Sylvii, but Faith and Robert have been to the apartment. Someone in the local public health agency called Faith to tell them of their grief counselling visit to our, Alain's and my apartment. She said there was room in the non-profit housing for me but we had to move now. I had told the public health nurse about what Faith and Robert had done with all my money and now public health resort to this maneuver. I feel threatened all the time. Faith said I must agree and sign over my bank account to pay any bills out of Alain's pension funds. So then Robert went on to say he blamed that friend Sylvii of your's for calling the police, as police called for appointments with Robert and Faith to discuss money losses from Alain's and my joint account, and so if I didn't agree and sign their bank paper, something bad might happen to me and then your friend, Sylvii will be blamed for everything. I was so scared Sylvii. They said they would frame you for everything that may happen to me." Carole said.

"Oh no," Sylvii said. "That public health nurse called me and I said I had already spoken to you about moving into any non-profit housing, and we were supportive of you through this period of grief and trauma at the bank. The nurse said she did not intend to be involved but felt this move to public housing good for you, Carole. Well, I told her that I spoke to you, Carole, and Carole has no intentions of moving, and intends on pursuing criminal charges against Faith and Robert for theft and using Alain's Power of Attorney for financial causes not medical causes."

We sat sipping our tea., "Robert called in again at my apartment too Sylvii. I mention this earlier because you are so ill these past weeks. He said you had been using your friendship with his father for years to be popular with the neighborhood. Can you imagine?"

"I am Sylvii's s friend because we moved into same neighborhood when we came to Missouri after you and Wallace had lived in neighborhood."

"I wish I had never moved to Missouri," said Carole.

"Where did you want to move to Carole?" Sylvii said. "I thought support from others here, like Carole and Alain, would be great for all of us after our oldest child, Gabriel, decides to move across many states for education. Alain showed so many kindnesses and said he felt so very bad for what had happened to me, a mother and such. We were friends only of course, and I thought his children, Faith and Robert so nice and supportive. You were away alot on your sales meetings or on the golf courses Wallace." Sylvii said.

Carole said, "There was nothing I could do so I signed the banking form."

Carole put her tea cup down and got up to leave and said, "I told the taxi driver to return in an hour. I must go soon."

"No Carole," Sylvii said. "I will call police again."

"Good-bye Sylvii," said Carole.

Carole walks to the doorway with Sylvii on her crutches, and following.

"I love you Carole," said Sylvii.

"Good-bye Sylvii."

A tall taxi driver stood smiling at the door and said, "Carole, Are you ready?"

"Thanks, yes," said Carole.

Sylvii followed on crutches out the door and down five stairs to see Carole slow and deliberate walking behind tall taxi driver to waiting car in driveway in front.

Turning back Sylvii walks back in through kitchen doorway to sit, and said, "I am calling the police."

"Sylvii," Wallace aid. "I am no good to you like this. What has happened here?"

"Oh get lost," said Sylvii. "Alain and I were friends but you have never been loyal and always blame me for losing Gabriel to his education.

Next day Sylvii calls state police office and asks to speak to state officer…

"She has moved to upper state Missouri but Drummond may be able to assist?" receptionist said.

"Drummond here,"

"This is Sylvii ….Bergeron calling. I reported a large theft on behalf of my friend Carole Laroque. I have been in terrible car accident and now Carole left my home minutes ago telling me she has been threatened by her children to move into government housing, and I have also been threatened if she does not cooperate. How can things have gone this far? I helped Carole move her account to my own bank at legal advice, and we together set up a joint account to help pay Carole's monthly rental costs and such. Now my bank has called too, and the bank teller, Janis told me Faith and Robert have been at bank with banking transfer form back to the bank where Carole's money was stolen. Carole of course and I feel so scared, she did not know what

—

else to do. Why have the police done nothing to help Carole?"

"I can be over to your home in twenty minutes Mrs. Bergeron.

"Fine, but please call me Sylvii," said Sylvii.

Sylvii got up from her living room sofa and on crutches went to front door to unlock door.

"Wallace," Sylvii said, "The police are arriving soon. Do you want to sit in?"

"No thanks," said Wallace. "I will take a walk."

Twenty minutes later State police Drummond arrives with knock on door.

"Come in," Sylvii said.

As the door opens, State police Drummond falls through the doorway into Sylvii's front entrance, and walking into living room seeing Sylvii said, "Hello, I am State police officer Drummond."

"Thank you for coming so quick," said Sylvii. "My husband has left for a walk. He is not involved in these issues with Carole although he knows the family well."

"Carole was here visiting yesterday. She has been taking a cab here as I cannot drive laid up with two broken legs. We have tea together and catch up on simple things, but now I cannot drive Carole to our mass for example she has begun to enjoy. Carole had fallen away from her church. Carole said Faith and Robert have been at her apartment with the banking paper, threatened her into signing and saying they will blame me, her friend, for all this trouble with the police."

"Have you advised Faith or Robert about our case," said Sylvii.

"No," said Drummond.

"I do not understand how things went this way." said Sylvii.

The public nurse dropped into see Carole in recent visit as she had developed a bad soar that needed treatment on her spine from an infection she somehow developed. I had met the nurse, kind of a trouble maker and interfering, but I told her I am loyal to Carole, her good friend. Friends are everything."

"Then this same nurse told me to butt out, and I needed to think of my own family, like husband and any children I have. So then I got a phone call from this same public health nurse who told me she had an opening at public seniors housing, and as Carole seems to be in such anxiety and might not be looking after herself well, she recommends Carole move to this facility. I asked this nurse what kind of place is this? Public Health requires Carole's pension funds to pay costs at facility. Can Carole go about the usual stuff, like going to mass together or picnics? I told Public Health to ignore Faith and Robert as they committed a crimes by theft by Power of Attorney from Carole's and Alain's joint account. This public health nurse advises public health prefer to by distant from these family issues, but must have funds to transfer Carole and take control of banking for public health costs."

"No," said the nurse "This government subsidized housing operates as closed ward for anyone with extreme anxieties like I have experienced with Carole, and with locked doors preventing trips to Mass or picnics or any outings to activities. To make things worse, the public health nurse said the government subsidy did not cover everything and she needed Carole's banking information and my cooperation to pay portions of costs," Sylvii said.

"Carole needs to be relocated?" Sylvii said, "as things seem beyond belief and any sense of our good lives we know."

"The police cannot help with relocation," said state police officer Drummond.

"My husband becomes of little use in this mess with our old friends," said Sylvii. "He thinks we should mind our own business. At this point I am scared. Look at me. I cannot even walk," said Sylvii. "The first officer Wilkins took all the information from me including the canceled checks Faith and Robert wrote on Carole's and Alain's account. I had to go back to that bank after speaking with her, police officer Wilkins and obtain the evidence. The first call I made with Carole to report the theft indicated the State's attorney's office were to receive the complaint as soon as possible. I never did a call. We went to my attorney to get advice and he revoked the Powers of Attorneys to Faith and Robert. But then somehow Robert or Faith got wind of the name of the lawyer, told Carole she had to go with them and get a new document drawn up. This lawyer then sent Carole an invoice for thousands of dollars. I asked Sylvii what happened. Carole said Faith and

Robert had come to her home and insisted on going to meet the attorney. We were only beginning to obtain documentation for Carole's new passport and travel to Europe. You know we are both French citizens." Sylvii said.

"Have you given any information from the police file to the district attorney's office? How did Faith and Robert find out about what lawyer I had known. We had done business together in past in my own commercial real estate practice," Sylvii said.

"No. There has not been any interference from Faith or Robert." said state police officer Drummond.

"What about Carole and Alain's cousin or friends in your office. Did anyone look at this file? I was cooperating with the police to gather any evidence. And now I have had all these injuries and look at me. My husband wants nothing to do with any of this. Our only child, Gabriel attends colleges out of state, and since years back and our marriage has never been easy ever since."

CHAPTER ELEVEN

Fine Print With Poetry

Album Fourteen Chocolate Eclairs

Olde Homestead Diaries

Sylvii lives alone now as Wallace left for California with his pal, Jacob. Sylvii reads all banking Information to Fern and cannot visit Carole any longer.

"I phoned to speak to Carole at her new location in closed ward. She cannot take calls, the manager said."

"I argued with this manager but she was very miserable about my visits to Carole," Sylvii said.

"I understand," Fern said. No, I do not want to visit either if I had to speak to Faith or Robert".

"Let us go over all these banking documents. How can anyone close an account with my name on it? We met with the bank manager. He said there were warning flags all over the account. No one should be able to access this money, including Faith or Robert," Sylvii said.

"Will Carole be fine?" Fern said.

"Carole's disappeared?" Sylvii said, "and I wonder if she went to France or became stuck away in public housing, Fern. This letter addressed to me arrived today I want to read to you like Carole speaks to us.

Dear Sylvii:

I regret not being able to share my news with you but everything has come together fairly quickly and now find myself deciding on relocating to Europe. Toulouse, France looks interesting and I have never visited the French Riveria. I have some acquaintances in these locations, so hope to meet with them over some coffee and such.

Everything in my world, and life, has taken a bad turn I cannot seem to correct. All the reporting to police and government agencies has done nothing to create my own security let alone correct wrongs. I have given up on getting any justice. So do not try to follow or reach me but I do hope one day we will be able to share some experiences together. I wish Wallace all the best, and do know you and he tried to lift my spirits many times. I hope you will be kind to each other and be strong for any unfortunate circumstances you do not continue to meet up with.

My children abandon me in their own mid life. Why, no one ever seems to know or understand these developments? Even so, I do feel justice must be served on children or anyone for that matter. Seems some priority given to them prevents me from finding any security, and lately even my own future and freedom threatened by Faith's belief government health services watch over me. Robert must have known how unfortunate these developments may seem, but in the process forgot to honor his parents, both Alain and myself. We stayed together as a couple because we follow our own oaths to honor and respect each other until death separates us. I no longer must honor this vow as Alain has now left me with passing away.

So Sylvii, I enclose my notes from experiences from purchase of the *Old Homestead* in Nebraska. I wish you well, and may your journey's take you to this magical place wherepeace and art combine to create one special harmony. Attached to my diaries for you to enjoy list few thoughts written in poetry I call our Chocolat Eclairs and with my Olde Homestead Diary, and my remaining gifts.

All the best, your dear friend, Carole.
CAROLE'S POETRY ALBUM

To dear pal, Sylvii,

Everything in my life takes violent turns I cannot seem to correct with all of our reporting to police and government agencies doing nothing to create my own security let alone correct wrongs of theft of Alain's and my joint financial funds. Loyalties seem to have disappeared from places I took for granted with my children and my community....so I have given up on getting any justice.

So do not try to follow or reach me but I do hope one day we will share some experiences together. I wish Wallace all the best, and do know you and he tried to lift my spirits many times. I hope you will be kind to each other and be strong for any unfortunate circumstances like as children abandon me for their own times, and in their own mid lives. With these brutal developments of theft of finances from Alain's and my accounts by children, even so, I do feel justice must be served on children or any one for that matter who strives to attempt or complete such violent actions of intimidations for my own daily life through actions unworthy of the family Alain and I raise together.

Although we, Alain and I, stay together as a couple because we follow our own oaths to honor and respect each other until death separates us I no longer must honor this vow as Alain has now left me with passing away. He never need have endured the abusiveness of Faith and Robert, or how they treated their own father.

So Sylvii, I enclose my notes from experiences from purchase of Old Homestead in Nebraska. I wish you well, and may your journey's take you to this magical place where peace and art combine to create one special harmony. Do not stay beyond nine days. After three to four days the place will be very harsh and even lonesome but peacefulness will arrive, promise to you. In the event you do not travel to Olde

Homestead I continue to wish you much success in all your future may assist you in striving to be and do.

Although, below fourteen poems and prose describe my deeper experiences for trying tocontinue on in the apartment I share with Alain, coping with Faith and Robert and developing daily life experiences on land I refer to as Olde Homestead in Nebraska. Writing prose or poetry supports me in this troubling journey, and now share with you as I depart our country and strive for better times. Best of luck, and know I love you always..

Your dear friend,
Carole.

—

Fourteen Chocolate Eclairs Poetry
Album by Carole Laroque

August Returning Alone

Soup Kitchens
Getting there early seems the thing to do
Gathering before opening is the respect
My gratitude is mine though
After a long while away.

My walk to the kitchen is far
My walk to the kitchen is near
Who comes?

The coffee is bad, but then coffee is
Sometimes having the cup of coffee
I believe
Finds a despair because I feel.

I smile to the other
A memory wall we have near
I do not forget maybe a kindness
To only say 'hello' is never lost.

For the conversation that begins
I got a dozen muffins but decided on croissants
He took bread and he said hopefully
Croissants are okay as you must like them.

—

Buying a croissant is extravagant
I know
But the bread is better because I dream.

Carole 11 pm.
02 September Second Roadtrip

31 August to Sagebrush

Hello Mr. Toad
You are very small
Unlike my toad from before
While pulling grass or weeds
From my long driveway
Dropping by seemed cute
As I wait
The visitor or neighbor.   *Carole 7:45 pm.*

03 September

Ripened Wheat
The field across is golden
Waiting for the harvest
Waving in the north wind
I thought of my old friend
Remembering our last visit
The sun has not sat
Returning to my ten acres
I begin to sweep
The thickest dirt, wood-shaving
into the 5 gallon pail;
To dump in a location
Through one path trodden.   *Carole 5:00 pm.*

German Blend

The instant blend is fine
For the early morning
I left with the desire
To continue the challenge
Is six quarter miles.   *Carole 7:20 pm.*

18 September

Introductions
The trip winds south
Worried I have not taken the turn north

I drive through the hills of my old youth
Nearby was my favorite bakery
Always full and very busy and I had to order;
I never know what to order;
So I was excited to see in my view
Running across the paved highway
The thick tail swinging behind
More silvery or tan than red
Fox Could blends the path to the north
And disappears into the hill
We met I say.   *Carole 10 pm.*

Third Roadtrip 31 August to Sagebrush Returning to Olde
Homestead

04 July Sunday Years Ago
My flight arrives at 4:30 pm. The plane was late from
Paris….I am invited to lunch; and We go to McDonalds.
Sylvlii must return to her home in nearby suburb leaves for
her bus. Fern invites me to stay on at her home in Missouri
until Friday. Carole.

18 July

Saved Wedding Cake
I asked the bride,
Could you save me a piece?

Frozen in the refridgerator freezer
Since;
Faith shares some wedding cake with her Mom
I am so grateful; The middle with icing-like cream is framme
I'd never heard the word before.   *Carole 6:15 pm.*

24 July
    Free Rootbeer
I had received the invitation
AW are celebrating
Saturday at 11 am is the street lunch
A variety of churches provide.
I decide to arrive ontime at 11 am.
As early means more time to sit with others
I hear the word hooker
I cannot hardly stand the sound
Nothing has happened
A security guard, a pretty blonde female, sits in a truck.

So AW rootbeer is heard
Five people had arrived
I am greeted with a wave
I stayed one hour for the extra large
She can only talk about her walk
In an alley as a Chinaman asks her to lunch
Her career is a wig stylist.
So I leave for home but alone walking home. Carole 6:30 pm.

27 July

Leaving the Location
Getting the paperwork complete
Was fairly simple
Meeting with others is ironic
Their melody of boredom rocks.　　　　*Carole 9:15 pm.*

Standing Brighter
They gather as one
Taller than before
Orange-yellow petals spread like ironed pillow cases
Be firm they holler I believe.　　　　*Carole 9 pm.*

02 August
Arrival
Visit is renewable
From a time of mistakes and misunderstandings
Visiting is thoughtful from rabbit holes of past
Together with two old friends.

Four and half hours later
Driving home to the season of a home
Emotions are troubled by indecision
Anticipating loneliness must be construed.
I remember He said my summit to a mountain;
Is my renewal....　　　　*Carole 7:30 pm.*

—

Sunday, 19 August
The Lone Goose
Fear is an odd emotion;
Going to my camping biodegradable toilet
Is an occasion to stargaze
Tonight on the return I hear in the trees
Harsh breathing sounds and I feel fear
I head into the tent;
Waiting ten minutes results in honk, honk, honk...
The Lone Goose gives notice to fly
The barn had been goose's rest.   *Carole 9:45 am.*

Tuesday, 28 August

Remembering the Black Angus

When I began my life leaving parents home
The friends I had thought this place well put
Leather chairs, dark subdued lighting
I invited my friend, who brought her friend
Changing my life did not change this friendship.

Returning has been like a relief of a tension
Emotions are unlocking;
Our past was riddled by the worst friend
Who held my husband's bachelor party
In the black Angus.
Drove us past but the name has changed;

*and I did not remember the hospital across the street. Carole
7:15 pm
I have practiced English as Foreign Language lessons for
style each day for fifteen to twenty minutes.   Carole
12:50 pm.*

12 September

Rest, Relaxation or Restoration

*The conditions are not relaxed
I'm getting a result,
Practice, practice, practice
How to rest or finding restoration.*

*My work on the Olde Homestead is continuous
Meeting the next challenge progressive;
Fiction or fantasy is the luxury
Leaky tent and clearing weary.   Carole 1 p.m.*

Olde Homestead Diaries

Evening Life is different now.

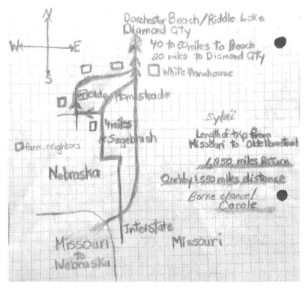

Carole Laroque's *Olde Homestead* Diaries
as bequeath to Sylvii Bergeron

—

21 August 1995

Carole....Sunset at eight in evening – light enough

I arrive at Olde Homestead Estate at six in evening. Tent set-up took about one hour with my prepared lunch meal another forty-five minutes. The trip was a bit far south on highway but the road was smooth and much less traffic. A bit of gravel on the secondary road was a problem but there was no traffic. The trip through Missouri towns seems different as I couldn't find the previous gas station but in town find very good Husky Station and AW worthwhile.

Few hours later, I drive through the town. Sagebrush seems a bit beaten-up with closedstorefronts, but friendly flags line the street. I didn't stop so as to arrive earlier at Olde Homestead and drive out of Sagebrush. I get excited when I try to spot the property as I left the interstate where oncoming traffic appears in my view before turnng left onto gravel. The gravel secondary road becomes rutted with recent rainfall and local traffic. Driving past enjoyable view of ripened wheat crops appears, and the crops ripen but no harvest.

As I arrive at turnoff with ditches full of tall grass, the property seems to feel like mineand I feel deflated as I see the clean-up ahead. The many purple milk thistle are in seed and seem to be imagine being able to pull them all. I see the toolshop and know I still want to try to clear and develop this building into some sort of art retreat like livable art studio.

—

Although processes look simple like sweeping and with carrying broken tool parts out of toolshop. Focusing on results of useable building keeps my motivations alive. Nearby, but beside tall caraganna hedge, inside tent seems restful and my plans to go to Diamond City tomorrow helps with directions from my last season's land broker.

As my Entrance Visa delays continue, I will try to stay remainder of August month into September with bringing warm clothes along in packing, and will try making coffee with propane stove. When I rest I hear alnight machinery harvesting nearby crops. These sounds provide some level of comfort I accept as sharing in this challenge of relocating to Olde Homestead in location I understand.

01 September

My first day did begin until 09:30 am. when I view one farm-size large, in unpainted boards, very old barn in more detail. I walk through the front door which I had not done before. The hanging door looks insecure so I choose only to walk in through back door. Front of barn seems to contain approximately six stalls. In between each stall is a curved fixture which sits about head level and looks like a very thick hook to hang a coat on. There is a valley walk-way or a long alley in front of the stalls resembling a feed or run-alley. The left side of the barn seems more compact than the right side. Possibly different types of animals were housed as in a mixed farming barn with pigs, chickens, horses and cows. The back of barn separates with three to four foot wooden wall from the front of the barn with the half wall. Any animals of past farming seem to leave the barn to the back pasture or yard area.

From back of the barn I access wooden slats forming barn ladder with steps nailed to the exterior wall to upper level of two-stories. I take pictures of upper level from the barn's concrete floor. To climb the ladder, I move a pole handle, like flat, rectangular shovel. Possibly the shovel was like a pitch fork to move hay around. I climb onto the barrier fence between the alley and last stall in the front section to step onto the first rung as the height of the ladder steps very high. Looking up into the second storey, bright tan-colored hard-wood flood appearing remains covered in hay. The hay still looks yellow. There are some floor boards missing so I hold the camera up through the floor opening to photograph the upper level. Returning camera and notepaper into my back, I climb down. I took a walk into the back yard smaller pasture area of barn feeling the exhaustion of visiting location. Barn oozes of historic past still seems to fill with farming comprehensive plan to house a variety of animals including maintaining upper-level hay loft. Walking out of barn towards barn's wooden slat back fence feel exhaustion of experience.

Leaving the country and keeping new ten acres property now I think of as Olde Homestead occurs to me.. I'm not sure of why but feel conflicting thoughts. Alain and I work years to establish a new life, in Missouri, after departing Nebraska, and someone else creates this interesting structure called a barn even with newer sheet metal roof to provide longevity in Nebraska.

1. *Do I want to sell the barn, develop the barn or sell the old wood become few issues?*
2. *I dream of renovations and plans for first level bathroom, kitchen, living-area and upstairs with at least two bedrooms in Olde Homestead barn.*

02 September 7 pm

In the next afternoon I took short drive to find Riddle Lake with eye-view from Olde Homestead, and about two miles from the driveway. Possibly an aluminum and very light canoe might have been carried to shore to lake nearby but now attracts wild fowl such as ducks and geese. In the drive down the one-lane, narrow, field road two hawks each sit kitty-corner from each other on fence posts.

The hawks sit still appearing large as footballs, grey with spots or splotches of whites. The farm road to Riddle Lake develops with waist-high ripened wheat and only a dirt road for single lane in the middle of nowhere.

04 September

After hot tea and cereal, I left for Dorchester Beach Resort at 11 am. Drive through Diamond City holds onto few memories from many years back when even I was in grade school as KFC revitalized in same corner location but Boston Pizza gone from main street location. Very few stores remain in downtown but for a large, recent supermarket mall development at Diamond City's edge. I see the McDonald's we celebrate Robert's 5th birthday. Friend at beach resort wonders how he would have enjoyed the McDonald cupcake sizzle candle I recall.

After arriving at Dorchester Beach Resort, I took a picture of the street our family cabincontinues to occupy and cabin sits on where the trees have grown. The old Riviere-Inn looksrenovated; looks cute like a cottage in blue siding and white roof. Getting closer begin to see how new owner adds rear french doors to large deck, and was in my old design plans had Alain and I remain in Nebraska.

More photos before stopping in front of neighbor's place. I see out-of-state plates. The owner appears from standing on her deck speaks up in very kind tones, and took time to tell me Carl passes on two months ago; other neighbor's in next block over towards beach gave them the news. I ask of details, and kind lady describes cancer and mixture of other things; but his wife fine........I give nice person my phone number, and I told her how much Carl dreams of visiting Asia. Our old friends sold cottage to them more than twenty years ago but stop in ten years ago to see the old place.

Carl's cottage still boasts wonderful attached deck with real painted thick log beams, and cottage sits like a small home. Once...I was invited to visit and enjoy comforts and compact kitchen Carl develops for his wife...... in U-shape with smaller sitting area looking through large picture window to resort black dirt lane in front. Two bedrooms to rear complete picture of quaint, lovely place.

After departing Carl's former cottage, I keep on with discovery going to the beach, for more photos and take out drawing tools to sketch. Notes recorded at eight in evening. Carole

—

Next Day: Clean-up in the tool shop entrance work area continues. I photograph sunshine through windows at eight-thirty in morning sunrise. Starting clean-up of building holding mystery of its past at eleven in morning, and finishing removal at two in afternoon all of the debris of dirt or broken tools and boards from right wall of left side of bulding to the pile outside but nearby in the field to left of building. The boards from broken door into bulding require cleaning and expose tongue-in-groove in solid wood, almost like oak. The boards may become useful to patch missing areas in walls.

Later, with brief fifteen minute drive to Sagebrush for only five miles or less distance, register to apply for new library card and find ability from librarian to order any book from three hundred libraries in Nebraska. After return drive to Olde Homestead, and small meal of bread and bananas, decide to rest for evening with sitting in car and warmth of sunset before retiring to sent set-up. I write notes resting in my sleeping bag Sylvii, and tonight write about loss of neighbor, Carl, from resort our family enjoy. Carl, who is older than Alain but still young enough, and tell a bit of his story I hope with photographs of Dorchester Resort and our friendly street of cottages. Carl loved the local Diamond City fair and ran the steam engine demonstration along with his son. This feature of summer vacations becomes greatest of times for Carl. Once I took Robert and Faith..... with me to see the demonstration as I stay longer at resort for

—

holiday, and Alain decides to return to our home in Missouri to attend to some work. Sunsets at eight in evening. Carole

05 September and 06 September

The workbench is 20 feet and First Sweep 07 September Slow morning to enjoy long breakfast in sunshine. Bagels and peanut butter taste fine while remembering emotional but joyful visits in memories of one past month since returning from overseas work in Asia.

We had visited and celebrated with extravagance of seeing food and craft exhibits.....in St.. Louis with Robert, Cheryl..and lovely granddaughter, Sonya,,,,,

Memories continue to stick with me like riding in the backseat with new granddaughter, Sonya, and watching her expressions for darkness in shock-dismay, but pleasant visiting with granma while I teach the new sound tsk...tsk.

15 September

My clean-up project does not begin until one-thirty in afternoon ending at four-thirty in afternoon.

The end of the week seems like the troubled Friday I've known. Banking issues where I have

been told bank will pay back money I shouldn't have paid, government agency who can't process a document requiring the possibility of a second trip to Valest..., and finally my oldest and closest friend from apartment building who moved shortly before Alain and I moved into building advising me the local state police do nothing as in her hands and tied to destroy a drug deal worth ten thousand dollars her sister makes, as her sister befriends others in drug business culture.

My seasonal home project seems important in a way of spending my time. Privacy is important in both places.

Final Visit to Olde Homestead August

Bird twitters everywhere, mostly south treeline. Arrive at two thirty in afternoon at Olde Homestead. Enjoy packed lunch. Three hours later finish tent set-up. Walk with carrying weights in either hand for physcial weight building to arm muscles....Quiet.

03 August
My Olde Homestead Acreage, Nebraska

Day 1: Last night's thunder and lightning rain storm starts at one in morning lasting until two-thirty in morning. Tent pegs hold and I stay dry. The bottom of the sleeping bag got wet as sits placed along the left wall from door. The puddles of water near the door sit downslope so did not bother me. The wind blows loud and strong knocking over the small water jug but all the tent pegs hold the tent and the tent fly stayed on top outside of tent. I place the tent about fifteen feet from the carraganna hedge and the north grove of poplar trees with the hedge hlod back the wind. Outside, the new five gallon compost pail toilet and lid were placed in front of the carraganna hedge and not disturbed by wind or rain storm. The recovered from garbage from home styrofoam seats did not blow away but the bag of old gloves soaked wet from rain. Everything else remains inside the car. Breakfast and dressing in my acreage clothes becomes struggle and physical effort. I feel like I want to be very lazy like the old days in the cabin at Riviera Beach, where neighbors nearby walk with friendly hellos. The sadness from my family's losses stays with me in memory of children, Faith and Robert staying close with me and memories of family life.

Sunshine and sounds from rustling trees on acreage invite me trying to ignite new memories. Pulling purple thistle today becomes to-be-made easy from drenching heavy rains. Seven-thirty in evening. Seven thirty in evening I sit in car in sunset and sunshine. Carole

Saturday, Day 02, 04 August

Light rain last night and today. Mosquitos big problem. After a cold breakfast of bread with fruit sauce, I put on my boots to walk to the storage sylo. I am relieved the interior seems undisturbed and the lock in place on exterior door. My push broom lays on the floor in front of me. The black and decker broom purchased first-summer on Olde Homestead from local hardware and gas station for twenty dollars. My Coleman three burner stove sits to the right of the door unharmed. The box seems damp but when removed to outdoors, seems fine. I'll take the stove back with me to store in dry place.

The long walk back to the toolshop now future liveable art studio completed and over but successful. I brought my own shovel from .....Missouri. Grateful I plan to prepare food to take the partial-used propane canister with care from *trunk, start-up propane to light the stove and heat my water for a cup of coffee. Light rains start. Then I put on my boots to clean-up some animal mess left – I'm not sure what – the mess is large pieces and one dead bird. I've begun to assemble tool shop items to photograph to try to sell to local Antique Dealer. Vintage food containers and tools may be valuable but after he sees photos, his answer becomes negative interest.*

Earlier today I remember my backpack for the hour daily walk plus twenty minutes. Supper is biscuits and sauce with half -bottle water. No sunset from roaming clouds. Helicopter passes low flying west this very quiet afternoon.

Carole....Seven-thirty in evening.

Sunday, Day 03...05 August

Rest and relaxation seem relevant today. Quieting myself from anxieties of unknown or being alone meet with small flying yellow birds high upon the power line disconnected to the toolshop. I look at the Old Homestead's barn and realize I want it to become reusable. So I will add these photos too for Antique Dealer in the hopes of a sale.

I wash my hair and sun myself. Black tea for breakfast is pleasant with bread and oatmeal. My food seems to be lasting the week. I prune driveway carraganna with small axe and pleased in my confidence. I've been doubting my decisions and for deciding France better option, then realize due to the experiences I had last year with Robert takinga my passport it was a good idea to hold out for more money. Going to Paris to work may be a future opportunity but I am trying to convince them the cost to travel not reasonable in my letter I must post later in Sagebrush... I put a bright green plastic strap on the door to toolshop.

So tomorrow I will photograph as much as possible. Getting large gallon oil can off the shelf is the biggest problem.

Two tuna sandwiches for supper extravagant as I use one can. It's odd how this simple existence becomes closer to my old life in Nebraska and Dorchester Beach Resort.

Thursday 09 August

Wednesday drove to Sagebrush for visit to Tax Collection and Assessment Office – Fifty Dollars for agricultural rates by cheque; Office provides gift of rural road map; I sign petition for Rural Funds for rural safety project. Then took a walk down mainstreet. Coffee Shop looks spiffy with new frontage upgrade. Small town mural designs across street are very attractive with concrete flower pots and petunias and new steel benches for resting. Even stop in at library where librarian with friendly questions asks advice about holidaying in Missouri. I suggest St. Louis her best choice.

Sagebrush grocery store I find busy with many customers. I buy groceries for thirty dollars – but not propane. Gas station sells no propane cylinders either – automobile gas costs become cheaper in Nebraska than Missouri. I took a different road back to Olde Homestead town and much shorter distances than five miles, only two miles – past local farm buildings –must turn left not right from my driveway

—

to drive over gravel roads to paved highway to Sagebrush –
plan to return to Sagebrush this same way.

After arriving at Olde Homestead cook two porkchops,
whole onion, cabbage – coleslaw. Big meal. Walk six times
down driveway. Twelve noon. Carole

Saturday 11 August

Friday becomes my disaster. Thursday afternoon I
smear soap over my face as an insect/mosquito repellant
which burnt my face and inflamed now red-eye. Mosquitoes
become thicker after last night's rainfall. I took it easy all
day – barely eating not cooking. Saturday was better; I
open the sleeping bag and slept as if in a bed. A sleeping
bag zipped-up making sleep uncomfortable, confining
my body so opening zipper like a blanket makes sleeping
possible.. There was a frightening windstorm in the night.
The wind came out of silence and like an ocean and very
noisy. The tent is holding together well. Saturday morning
I ate a banana and bun with juice and left for the market
in Diamond City.

However, clerk at hardware store indicates farm
markets will be Thursday. So I hope I will plan well and
return next Thursday. The grass in ditches cut by road
maintenance late this afternoon seem to be one foot wide
but an improvement from waist-high grasses in front of
property late this afternoon – but maintenance only cut the
grass bordering front of the driveway exposing the entrance
to the gravel road..

I took some pictures at Riveria beach to share with Sylvii….later….

Tuesday, 14 August

Monday is cloudy. I need a rest. The water almost gone. After a piece of bread, a hotdog bun and banana and vitamins, I drive to Sagebrush gas station to ask for water. They fill my five gallon water tank and small container for free at the garage. After I drove down main street to the Return Bottle Depot discover centre opens at one-thirty Monday to Friday. I keep plentiful supply of juice boxes to stimulate my sugar on Olde Homestead, but like to leave behind before my return trip.

The Coffee Shop looks open nearby and enjoy soup and sandwich and coffee for six dollars, and chat with owner about life in Thailand, China or France. Later I drove around to local motel for the information if decide conditions to harsh for tenting….

First thing this next morning, repeat drive to Sagebrush to buy food. Bought groceries to last the trip and cost about thirty-two dollars and another container of bug spray repellant. Mosquitoes continue to be very thick with high grasses in ditches helping to promote reproduction of pesty insects.

Wednesday, 15 August

The day develops very quiet. No harvest nearby. Smoke from northern fires send smoke around and back to area but mosquitoes and black flies continue. Bug spray helps reduce size of bites. I move breakfast location to behind car and I rest against the trunk's bumper. I took my full coffee cup and lawn chair to clear activity area I now call garage. While sitting in my sole folding chair, notice underfoot of thick layers of dirt small portion of concrete forming pad of former garage to Olde Homestead.

My plan to climb the wall ladder on side wall of garage changes, and move to adjoining room with work bench that forms the tool shop. I knock down the linoleum ceiling in shop with a pole instead. I continue shoveling and moving tool boxes until three in afternoon. I took lunch at two in afternoon.....tuna on hotdog buns and one fresh peach fit my hunger needs. Taking rest and nap in car late in afternoon becomes necessity but treat to me. The smoke and mosquitoes are too thick to walk outdoors in or down gravel road viewing fields of wheat or barley. Getting a bit more rest seems okay.

Friday, 17 August

The heavy due is less. Breakfast in sunshine is comfortable but I now can take my lawn chair and instant coffee to the garage to sit inside away from mosquitoes. A few bees fly by. I think the wire and nails continue to be a hazard. Washing some underwear in a basin and sunshine is almost normal as I witnessed in Thailand. I don't have to deal with student or walkers as was situation. The experience revealing to me how I am judged and judge myself becomes subjective.

I drive to Diamond City Walmart at ten-thirty in morning. Using Walmart's bathroom and looking at travel suitcases passes time for enjoyable shopping excursion. I am stunned by the amount of traffic. The MacDonald's restaurant is nearby where we spent Robert's birthday, his fourth birthday with sparklers. The market begins at four in afternoon. I drove to Diamond City Downtown, park my car and walk a bit and found Diamond City library. They will let me tutor adhoc English as Second Language Monday, Tuesday evenings next spring, summer. So I've completed the logistics for payingr rental fees. I left for the farm market at four in afternoon. It's nice, easy to find, few stalls, and I receive the information to call if I choose to sell any homemade tie die or prints. I bought honey-made lip and skin balm in lemon grass from lady who had lives locally but farms fifty miles away, and buy two cobs of corn. Seven o'clock in evening Carole.

Bird Watching I
19 August Journal

1. 15 August, Wednesday at 10:00 am

Bright, completely yellow small bird perched on purple flowering thistle blossoms. Siting is less than five minutes in large field but in front and near the carraganna hedge beside well....drinking instant coffee in vintage garage; sitting on a lawn chair. One bird like-a-canary perches across the driveway approximately one hundred feet directly in front of my chair.

2. 18 August Saturday at 11:00 am.

While preparing my breakfast, a yellow midsize bird sat perched on an old dismantled power line between barn and pole beside ancient well-house. The bird fluffs wings to expose black on the underside The singing lasted at minimum five minutes. The bird flew directly west, slightly north in cuve towards the corner large poplar trees of property frontage. No similar birds flocked. Unsure of nature and name of bird.

3. 20 August--The Olde Homestead Barn
A few pails of straw and dirt easily clear the stalls. Sweeping will tidy the stalls enough to move the contents of toolshop. The barn is ideal for wreath-making if ever try craft again.

4. Second removal of moss from two of three vintage shop doors clears the bottom of Right-Door. There is an opening and daylight to shop. The Left-Door is in better shape but grass problem is serious. Seven in evening. Carole.

Tuesday, 21 August

Slept until 08:30 am alarm. Cold at middle of night is hard on sleeping. Long breakfast until 11:30 am. Left for Sagebrush Returns-Depot..net $3.80 with few picked-up tins. Friendly service. Filled five gallon water at Gas Station before going to Public Library. Atmosphere is homey-like welcoming. Shop at grocery store to cook big supper of porkchop, coleslaw and cauliflower. Walk in sunset with

singing songs out loud to quiet countryside fields of corn,
wheat and farmer's choice. Carole at seven in evening

Wednesday, 22 August; Thursday, 23 August

A new sketch for Yellow Autumn Leaves in the am.
helped me to feel grateful to newly discovered. Wild Buffalo
Bean flower patch beside the/my new path to Barn. I
weeded out thistle to discover the number of flowers
increasing. Removing all the wild dandelion next.
Sweeping stalls of Olde Homestead Barm I complete on left
of front entrance for storage of vintage pieces/parts ...from
machinery. Carole

Thursday, 23 August

Early this morning at one o'clock, I woke sleeping in
the tent;

Friday, 24 August

The weather is cold and windy. I had banana sandwich,
cookies and a juice box for breakfast before leaving for
Diamond City and Timmies for coffee. and time to prep
for visit to Public Library opening at twelve-thirty in
afternoon and Library staff welcoming visitors.

Sunday, 26 August
Written For Saturday 25 August

Heavy rain in the night created a very wet ground making weed and grass pulling extremely easier. The tool shop front is clear within six feet but low grass exists. I started the West Side with thick dark grass and lifted the grass previously walked on. Last year's grass causes a problem of ground sticking and even rodent holes (possibly) so should not be left but moved to a compost location. Sorting contents in removable salvage is possible. Two boxes, one with glass, one with vintage oiling tools I remove, clean, for possible sale. The remaining contents will be stored in Barn. One thirty in afternoon. Carole

Believing in the pace of the final stage of storing contents in Barn helps me decide to gather all grass and weed clippings to one central location, where the car remains parked and grass trampled. The two piles of dirt from Vintage garage sat nearby very close to my cooking had to be shoveled to a new location across the main driveway. I had been cooking next to this very contaminated-looking soil. These two tasks took three hours. The sunset can be seen and sets at seven-forty-five in evening.

Monday, 27 August

Shopped in Sagebrush ....and Walmart...hardware chain store for any help with compost bags. Stop for Library time. Bought sausage to cook!

Carole....Seven-thirty in evening

Tuesday, 28 August
Bird Watching II

—

Eleven-thirty in morning: Flock of the small yellow birds, I think are warblers or so been told, visit carraganna hedge across driveway beside well pump. Wax-wing came out of caraganna on corner of well house to perch.

Twelve noon: All flew diagonal south or one yellow flew west. They all disappeared by 12:00 noon.

Warbler is covered in most-bright-yellow with small-grey spot;

Waxwing is red-grey colour with black head and brim-like-hat;

Wednesday, 29 August

Much warmer last night. The tent was comfortable. Left for Real Canadian Oil Change at 10:00 am but found out the car requires motor work for $250 for motor thermometre and reminding me how poor and too foolish or not able to afford to drive to Abbotsford for a job appointment.

Maybe I can work a deal for costs; go to Paris; go to Dublin; go to Thailand; go to China.

Thursday, 30 August

For third day this week, I drive to Sagebrush to complete car repair. Repair took ninety minutes.

I took a walk to the nearby local Mission, and asked to meet the Pastor I asked if I could stay for lunch and, "Yes," he said, "Soup and sandwich." Pastor is the Manager and there is only one service a week on Sunday. Pastor asks of my paying work in English as foreign language and work history. I told him of my acreage and hoped he would visit in the future. The car repair seems a success.

Carole....Seven in evening

Friday, 31 August
Bird Watching III Four-forty-five in afternoon:

One yellow bird with grey chest, maybe a warbler, flew alone to carragannas. Last evening was warm and same birds were perching lower in carraganna hedge beside decompost five gallon pail fifteen feet from tent.

The front lawn is emptying as I sort to store in barn. The ceiling linoleum is planned as tent pad in garage for next visit. The wind is strong and has blown tent fly off yesterday and today. The row of north poplars is turning gradual shades of yellow. While moving and digging with shovel, moss from the north side of toolshop, I found the concrete lip to foundation that would have been the carpenter's from Olde Homestead efforts to seal the base. I'm planning to create a six foot wide grass free perimeter around toolshop.

Sunday, 02 September Saturday

I attend Diamond City Farmers Market. The weather was cold with rain, only ten stalls with vegetable, teas, soaps, deodorants. T-shirts could fit in, – wonder about cost to attend? I did not talk to anyone. Heavy rain in afternoon caused temperature to drop, very cold last night. I'm completing moving toolshop contents to Barn from lawn, – but shop still needs clearing. Maybe I'll finish. Last

—

night at 10:15 pm brilliant sky fills with stars and Milky Way above horizon to horizon.

01 September Labor Day Sunday

I'm eating lunch at Beach picnic tables, tuna sandwiches. I'll take a walk down the Beach, take photos of colors, and streets. Windy and warm weather encouraged me.

Carole....One in afternoon

Monday, 03 September

While at resort beach calls to request a visit. Her and husband follow me out on way back to Olde Homestead to delivered the interior door I bought for one dollars from garage sale. They tour the acreage; look at contents— did not ask or take anything;

Two-thirty to three in afternoon They left at five in afternoon. Very sunny.

Next Day. No birds in morning; No birds at eleven in morning.

Rain began overnight — stayed all day. Turning Left at driveway is the easier drive this year to Sagebrush. Gas station provides free water. I bought three dollar hot dog with water for lunch; use garage bathroom, bought gasoline; third fill-up at Sagebrush Gas and one at Esso station equals four fill-ups of gasoline to equal quantity to drive to acreage from Missouri. Sitting in warm car passes the afternoon.

—

Tuesday, 04 September

Last night temperature went to zero degrees but frost obvious. Very cold and hard to sleep. I went to Sagebrush Library; weather is to warm to seventy-five degrees with lows to forty-five degrees to forty-eight degrees.

The garage is colder so I'm not convinced any longer I can put the tent inside. I should finish up soon and prepare to leave on the Tuesday, 18 September. Sun has almost set in twenty minutes. Carole 7:15 pm

Wednesday, 05 September..

Getting up at six in morning, I saw frost on the tent zipper flap and walked out into a layer of frost on everything, even the car. I slept off and on with strange nightmares of spending times with my Dad. I felt a bit jumpy and thought the very large bumble bee was inside the tent but was sitting on the tent wall outside in morning sunshine. The sky was blue with a first slice of a new moon in the east.

1. *First thing is to wash underwear;*
2. *Soak feet in used water;*
3. *clean toenails;*
4. *wash car with used water;*
5. *wash hair; Method: put basin on hood with two cups cold water, shampoo twice and condition.*

The sun shone with much warmth so I made a huge lunch. I used the dirty water to take road dirt off car and bugs. One fried porkchop, corn on cob, four potatoes, two slices of Italian bread with coleslaw are cooked, eaten and hair dries all sitting in warm sunshine.

At three in afternoon have to begin chores.

I drive to Sagebrush public phone booth to make phone call to follow through with register complaint of financial losses to adult children ....with FBI...and Missouri State Police,.... and State prosecutor offices ...with results but decline my application for prosecution to return money lost.

I walked up to metal round sylo granary to replace items I photograph when I arrive seems to take three hours but there many to put away. The 7-Up bottle has been removed from them for deposit, which has gone well in Sagebrush.

I haul the largest items from front yard to barn; long sharp triangle shape steel part; long board, long metal narrow panel. As I had done self maintenance most of the day I decide to sit in sun to finish the watercolor; Carole. Seven-forty-five in evening

Thursday, 06 September

Emptying decomposable toilet is heavy work but without this toilet, these four weeks would not be possible. Carole Seven-thirty in evening.

Friday, 07 September

Heavy windstorm collapses the tent. The wind is from east and no tree barrier. Starting at ten in evening. Storm lasting until nine in morning. I had to leave the collapsing tent at seven-thirty in morning. I wore my pjs for first time to car, (or maybe second) and change to make oatmeal bread, orange and coffee. There was a very wide streak of lightning across the north sky, thunder and heavy downpour from nine-thirty in morning to eleven in morning. I change clothes, jeans, sweater, to attend the invitation to lunch from local farmer in area. Nice to be accepted locally I feel, and visit Diamond City. Lunch of bacon and lettuce and tomato sandwiches, terrific black tea from a vintage brown betty and cinnamon buns with ice cream. Later shop at local Walmart before stopping into visit family friend, Shirley, friend to her and elder granma, who is ninety-nine years young. What a treat. We stay-a-bit, with Shirley, and share in Shirley's box of turtle chocolates, and I held her hand to thank Shirley. What a sweet capable woman. Her health seems very good but sits in a wheelchair or stands with her walker. Later we drive to store before leaving Diamond City. This day was tops off with a visit to a two-storey thrift shop with decent prices and good stock.

"I'm sleeping in a field in a tent on an original Olde Homestead," said my Diamond City friend.... to Shirley.

"She's alone out there," Shirley said.

Saturday, 08 September

Sunshine and the tent held. I liked the small sausages and washed underwear, soaked feet, wiped off car. Two hours of moving tools to barn results in color locations of red, green, blue, orange that illustrate their company ie. From vintage era 1913. Practicing each night with walk seems normal and the effortless. Carole

—

Sunday, 09 September

Windy night from west does not destroy the tent. Sun at eight in morning warms the tent. I sleep but had to fix the fly at two in morning. All day I spent clearing the yeard of toolshop contents I had thrown out to clean and store in Barn. My large breakfast of half package small sausages, oatmeal, two potatoes, four slices bread, banana and coffee keeps me content. My practice for tutoring English as Foreign Language topic of animals was more effective tonight; Mystery to me becomes why accept the isolation from this Olde Homestead project for new result. I feel less inhibitions.

Carole..... Seven o'clock in evening.

Invitations to meet or visit in Diamond City or Sagebrush lessen isolation.

Monday, 10 September,

I went to car in PJ's at eight-thirty in morning. The tent held off the rain. Tonight I feel fear of this and anxiety but have cleared the front yeard tonight. I plan to leave next Tuesday. Weather forecast is bad. Lawyer called me asking for fees so I referred them to land broker. I never hire anyone or sign anything.

Seven-fifteen o'clock in evening

Tuesday, 11 September.

.Morning arrives at six o'clock in morning, with no wind, no rain, and heavy dew. Weather forecast below

—

forty degrees overnight to thirty-eight degrees. Daytime temperature comfortable.

Bird Watching....observe magpie....Animal Watching ..observe black cat.

The final complete move of toolshop to Barn of the contents from underneath toolbench, table, and floor is today. Only tidying up left. The toolshop continues to require final ten percent sorting and sweeping. A new plan must be developed. I can start stomping on grass around perimeter to create clear border to allow painting. Even caragannas are turning. A black cat and a magpie appeared today. The black cate peered into the garage where I was enjoying green tea. One magpie swooped the entire yard, perched in barn briefly, and left..

Seven o'clock in evening

I complete my second watercolor and thrilled to paint under these conditions.

Wednesday, 12 September

Intermittent cloud and rain until eleven-thirty o'clock in morning results in downpour lasting an hour and more. My fifth week on homestead seems like a lengthy time but I feel grateful for any progress. Clearing has gone well with barn location. If contents are useful to anyone, the contents are simple to view. Two stalls of Barn are used with a third small stall large pieces and tool parts.

I have practed online English as Foreign Language lessons and style each day for fifteen to twenty minutes. Twelve-fifty o'clock in afternoon Carole

—

12 September

Leaky tent and clearing weary.
Carole... one o'clock in afternoon

Thursday, 13 September

The night was quiet, colder with fog this morning prevented the building or trees from visibility. Breakfast is long with tea and decompost day seems easier. Five weeks has past. I can see progress. Drove to Sagebrush for Returnables. Receive two dollars with good service, and friendly. Stopped in at Library, and caught up on papers from home.

Plan to leave Olde Homestead next Wednesday, 19 September,

Rain and cold weather are forecasted. I've christened toolshop studio today. I believe the room earned the title. Seven o'clock in evening Carole

Friday, 14 September

Although very cold, rain and wind held off. I slept intermittently. Getting up at eight o'clock in morning; dressing in tent, completing physiotherapy and cooking breakfast consumes me. One black-yellow breasted bird perched on wire at eleven o'clock in morning. Clean the Stedler vintage wood stove so I began clearing the SE corner of garage of glass broken from the two fallen windows laying in dirt and one double paned window still unbroken. Clearing of stove and floor lasts two hours after storing the last of the toolshop in Barn. I enjoyed the beef stir fry and

cooked outside. *Temperatures thirty-five to forty degrees..*
Carole

NOTE; *One Week after Labor Day weekend is absolute
latest to leave. Weather can change very quickly. Recovering
in two-day hotel stay. Avoid Sagebrush Hotel if decide
to leave; Get on highway to north Nebraska or return to
Missouri for best choice. Stayed at Olde Homestead five and
one half weeks in great. Progress made to pitch tent in garage
and cook under cover of garage. Standing in the building
after clearing rubbish and dirt come to surprise benefit of
discovering building authentic vintage Olde Homestead
garage.*

Saturday, Sunday 15, 16 September

*Weekend. After break in Garage, the box of broken
window glass is packed for disposal. A stop-off at bird
sanctuary and tourism is encouraging as a future activity
and is open nine to five Monday thru Friday. I dumped the
box in bin near Transfer Station in Diamond City. Baking
soda is needed due to instant coffee seriously staining my
teeth. At the Diamond City Public Library sit in foyer as
too noisy. I meet a younger man at the seating area. He had
quit his farming job and was giving away his groceries. He
gave me soya milk and chocolate. I suggested he stay in local
free-hostel as he had ten pound hamburger in one pound
bags to donate.*
*Ten pm., and I wake to the loud east winds and a wet
pillow and jacket. I have to move into my car. I start the*

car twice for warmth. This morning, I am staring out at our family tent drying in the wind after moving contents to Vintage Olde Homestead Garage. I feel gratitude towards this tent for all the years of family camping so the tent is dragged to Vintage Garage and at two o'clock in afternoon complete move to interior location.

Never again will anyone be able to say, "Carole sleeps in a field." about life and times on the Olde Homestead..

I drive to Sagebrush to gas-up and bought their deli sandwich for five dollars, which is cut in half for two suppers. I'll have to sleep in car as the sleeping bag and jacket are still wet. I must look into the laundromat.

Saturday morning at ten-thirty o'clock to eleven o'clock in morning.

Bird Watching A full size hawk circles the North yard to fly with wings outspread into the tree line. Later, on the drive to....Diamond City, hawk circles over the highway.

Seven-thirty o'clock in evening

FOR NEXT YEAR:

Dear Sylvii The diaries contain frightening adjustments and survival style living but the experiences do reveal to ourselves our propensity to adjust to adverse environments at any cost. I do hope we meet-up in Paris in next year or two…You will not be able to reach me easily, however, I can find you. I am indebted for your help in solving these dilemmas with mine and Alain's accounts, and surely wish your accident never happened and for your speedy recovery... love Carole.

PostScript. July 1997...Good luck Sylvii, and may our times be known...Please enjoy my poetry I wrote while on the land of the *Olde Homestead*. Your encouraging words to write was the main factor in my being able to write to you and decide on leaving USA for France... All the best, and may our futures be bound. Together in our dedications to each other and for honest dealings from anyone...family or others....Sylvii..Please read my poetry too with my Olde Homestead diaries..........

THE END..........

Printed in the United States
by Baker & Taylor Publisher Services